An
Intolerable
Burden

BY THE SAME AUTHOR

Painting Water
Waterloo, Waterloo

An Intolerable Burden

Teresa Waugh

HAMISH HAMILTON

London

HAMISH HAMILTON LTD

Published by the Penguin Group
27 Wrights Lane, London W8 5TZ, England
Viking Penguin Inc., 40 West 23rd Street, New York, New York 10010, U.S.A.
Penguin Books Australia Ltd, Ringwood, Victoria, Australia
Penguin Books Canada Ltd, 2801 John Street, Markham, Ontario, Canada L3R 1B4
Penguin Books (N.Z.) Ltd, 182–190 Wairau Road, Auckland 10, New Zealand

Penguin Books Ltd, Registered Offices: Harmondsworth, Middlesex, England

First published in Great Britain 1988 by
Hamish Hamilton Ltd

British Library Cataloguing in Publication Data

Waugh, Teresa
An intolerable burden.
I. Title
823'.914[F]   PR6070.A9/

ISBN 0–241–12352–6

Typeset at The Spartan Press Limited,
Lymington, Hants
Printed in Great Britain by
Butler and Tanner Ltd, Frome and London

For Sophia, Alexander
Daisy and Nathaniel

We . . . are heartily sorry for these our misdoings; The remembrance of them is grievous unto us; The burden of them is intolerable.

Book of Common Prayer

CHAPTER I

It was the handsome postman again today. The one whose brother was also a postman, but the brother was not nearly so good-looking. Nancy Potter looked down at the sink. She and her husband George had just finished breakfast and she was washing up. Her hands in the washing-up water looked coarse and red. She never wore rubber gloves as they made her clumsy, so despite the years of care she had spent on her hands and the money she had spent on creams, time had taken its toll. She washed the last saucer and placed it carefully on the draining board before pulling the plug out of the sink, wiping her hands on the flowered apron which her daughter, Claire, had given her for her birthday and glancing again out of the window.

The postman was just shutting the garden gate, whistling like all good postmen should as he did so. Nancy wondered what he would look like without his cap. The handsome postman always wore his cap. Perhaps he thought it suited him. It occurred to Nancy that anyway he probably looked better in uniform than he did in his own clothes which she imagined might be rather nasty. She could just see the top of his head over the hedge as he walked up the path to number 33 next door. I wonder, she thought, what he looked like naked. Did he have a hairy chest? Was his body perhaps a little too white . . . ?

'I'll fix that door handle now if you like.'

Nancy jumped out of her skin at the sound of George's voice and she felt the blood rush to her face. She quickly snatched a cloth and began to dry the cups and saucers. Supposing George could read her mind. But of course it was ludicrous to worry about that – for one thing there was no question of his being able to read her mind and for another he would never in a thousand years imagine that she had been daydreaming about the postman. But still she felt rather ashamed. It was perfectly ridiculous and rather digusting of her to be thinking about naked postmen at her age. Or at any age for that matter. Times had certainly changed – bad language and naked bodies were to be heard and seen on television every day, sexual morals among the young had altered radically since her day, homosexuality of which Nancy had only the dimmest understanding was publicly condoned, the most intimate details of people's private lives were discussed in the press and yet it was still profoundly shocking for a woman in her late fifties to be thinking about a naked postman. Nancy was sure of that and she felt suitably guilty, but at the same time annoyed at her guilt.

'I can't quite understand what's wrong with this thing,' said George. He had a screwdriver in his hand and was tinkering with the door handle. 'Ah, that's better,' he said, peering closely at what he was doing and turning the screwdriver with determination.

Nancy looked at him. He was really quite irritating at times, George. From the look of concentration on his face anybody would think he was engaged in splitting the atom, not just tightening a loose door handle.

Behind George, on the corner of the kitchen table, lay a pouch full of screwdrivers neatly arranged in order of size. One was missing from somewhere in the middle of the range.

'Well, there we are,' said George straightening up. 'I think that's just about done the trick.' He returned the screwdriver he had been using to its allotted place and began to roll the pouch up neatly.

[2]

'That won't be giving you any more trouble now,' he said in tones of deepest satisfaction.

Nancy felt a further surge of irritation. Good Lord, she could have mended the thing herself for two pins. Then she felt guilty again. Poor George. She was being a bit unfair – after all she had asked him to mend the beastly door and traditionally – ever since their marriage more than thirty years earlier – George had mended things about the house.

'I think I heard the postman,' she said and hurried from the room.

'Just a postcard from Claire,' she said, coming back into the kitchen. The message on the back of the postcard read: 'Having a super time, gorgeous weather, lovely pizzas and masses of Chianti. Love Claire.' Nancy looked at the picture on the other side. It was of Michelangelo's David. She found herself blushing and thinking of the postman again as she handed the card to George.

'What a long time these cards take to get here,' George remarked. 'She must have been back for at least a week, hasn't she?'

It was Saturday morning and Claire had in fact been back at work all that week although she hadn't yet seen her parents. She and her boyfriend, Francis, with whom she lived, were coming over for Sunday lunch the next day.

Nancy glanced at the kitchen clock. It was getting late. She must hurry up and go to the shops before they became too crowded. Shopping on Saturday mornings was always a hassle.

It looked like rain so Nancy put on her mackintosh. She felt in the pocket to check that she had a scarf in case it rained and then she took her 'shopper' and wheeled it away to the front door, called goodbye to George and was off down the path and on to the shops.

As she walked Nancy thought about Claire. She hadn't seen her for a while and was looking forward to hearing her news. She wondered what Claire would like for lunch tomorrow, and then she began to think about Francis. Nancy could not for the life of her think why Claire and

[3]

Francis didn't get married. They had been living together for five years – ever since Claire was twenty-three. It certainly didn't seem as if Claire would ever look anywhere else now. She and Francis were already like an old married couple. As for Francis, there was certainly no likelihood of him finding someone else. He was far too dependent on Claire. In fact she had rarely seen a young man so dependent. Francis was two years younger than Claire and was still in his last year at London University when they began living together. There had been a terrible to-do when he failed his engineering degree. His father had blamed Claire which was absurd as Nancy could remember how concerned Claire had been at the time. She had known all along that he hadn't been doing his work and had done her best to urge him on. Poor Claire had certainly thought in those days that she could make him work for her sake but of course she had been wrong. But give the devil his due, it was hardly his fault that he was a chronic asthmatic – that certainly didn't help. It must be a worry having to live on pills. Poor boy.

In fact Nancy thought that far from blaming Claire, Francis's father ought to be grateful to her for supporting Francis in every way – both financially and emotionally.

Nancy reached the greengrocer's shop on the corner. There was already quite a long queue which she joined as she went on musing about her daughter. She was sure that Claire would like to have children and even in these modern times, if you were going to have children, it was surely better to marry.

George of course took a typically masculine attitude to the matter. He had said what needed to be said at the start; now he thought, and often told Nancy abruptly, that although he didn't approve of Claire and Francis living together there was nothing he or Nancy could do about it. If that was how they wanted to live then it was up to them. They should be left alone to get on with it.

When at last Nancy's turn came she bought five pounds of potatoes, a Savoy cabbage and a pound of carrots.

[4]

Nothing in the shop looked very exciting this morning and as she left the greengrocer's it began to rain quite hard. She was glad of her scarf which she pulled from her pocket and tied round her head before making her way across the road to the butcher's shop. Shopping was dispiriting at the best of times and it seemed to take particularly long that morning. When she eventually reached home again she found George fast asleep in an armchair in the sitting room. *The Times* newspaper was open and spread over his face. It fluttered faintly as he snored. His arms hung loosely over the sides of the chair and some loud music – probably by Dvořák – resounded from the radio on the table beside him.

George was perfectly extraordinary. He was quite like a teenager in his capacity for sleep. How on earth could he sleep with all that noise going on anyway? That man could sleep all day, although Nancy supposed that he must have cleaned the car before going to sleep. George always cleaned the car on Saturday morning. If he was so exhausted all the time then it was just as well that he was due to retire at the end of next year. Nancy left him sleeping in the sitting room and went into the kitchen to unpack her shopping and to heat up some soup for lunch. She and George, when he was at home, always ate soup for lunch and after the soup they had an apple or a banana and a cup of coffee. Perhaps a biscuit or two. Nancy made excellent home-made shortbread. They ate their main meal in the evening except, of course, on Sunday.

After lunch George took the dog for a walk while Nancy ironed some shirts. By the time George came back Nancy was longing for a cup of tea. When she had emptied the teapot and washed up the cups and saucers she took out her knitting and sat down to watch television until it was time to cook the supper. George sat down beside her on the sofa with *The Times* carefully folded ready for him to do the crossword. By the time he had done the first anagram and solved an easy clue about cricketing he had fallen fast asleep again. *The Times* slipped to the floor, his spectacles slid down his nose as his head lolled back and his mouth fell open. Nancy gave him a sideways glance and turned her attention back to the television. The dog at George's feet slept as soundly as its master.

On Sunday morning when George had taken the dog out he went as usual to the local church. George was a creature of habit and for him Sunday wasn't Sunday if he had not been to church. At times over the years Nancy had wondered if George really believed all that stuff and occasionally she had questioned him. George never ceased to be amazed that Nancy should question his faith. Like a child he blindly believed in the teaching of the Bible down to the last detail. He didn't just believe in the fundamental Christian truths of the Resurrection of Christ and the Virgin Birth, but he believed in Adam and Eve and the Serpent and that Noah had filled his ark with two of every species, he believed that Elijah went up to heaven in a chariot and that Lot's wife was turned into a pillar of salt. He argued that if Christ was born of a pure Virgin and if He rose again from the dead on the third day, then anything could be true and if you were going to believe in any one part of the Bible then you might as well swallow the whole lot from Genesis to the Book of Revelations and be done with it.

As for Nancy, she had no time for any of that. It would be nice to be able to believe, she supposed, but none of it seemed very likely to her although, for the family's sake, she used to go to church at Easter and Christmas when the children were small. Now she was glad to get George out of the house for an hour or so on Sunday mornings so that she could tidy up and get on with the cooking in peace.

Nancy prepared an excellent Sunday lunch of roast beef and Yorkshire pudding, roast potatoes, carrots and cabbage with gravy and horseradish sauce, and for pudding she had made a lemon meringue pie. Lemon meringue pie had always been a favourite of Claire's.

Claire and Francis arrived at half-past twelve. George and Nancy were delighted to see them.

'You both look wonderfully brown,' said Nancy as George poured glasses of sherry for them all.

'We had a super time, we really did,' said Claire. 'Neither of us wanted to come back one bit. Did you get my card?'

Claire was delighted to see her parents and to tell them all about her Italian holiday. For a long time after she and Francis began to live together Claire had hesitated to come home. She had felt her parents' strong disapproval of Francis however hard they tried to hide it.

In any case they had not always tried to hide it. At first George had taken Claire aside and given her a lecture on Christian marriage. He found it hard to accept the fact that his daughter, who had been brought up in a strictly moral background, was living openly with a man to whom she was not married. Not that he had particularly advocated marriage to Francis. On the contrary. The boy was far too young and had no job, no prospects, and apparently little desire even to look for a job.

At the time Claire had found it quite difficult to defend Francis. She could see that from her parents' point of view he was hardly the ideal partner for their darling daughter and she could scarcely expect them to appreciate Francis's perfect sweetness and painful vulnerability. So she just used to tell them that Francis really was looking for a job and that she was sure that he would soon find something which suited him, and if he could do that he would be bound to work hard and to succeed at whatever he tried. With half her mind she believed what she said, for Francis, she knew, was intelligent, sensitive and imaginative. All he lacked was self-confidence.

At one stage Francis was taken on by a bedding firm but unfortunately, surrounded as he was by all those mattresses, his asthma became so acute that he had been obliged to give up the job. Claire felt very sorry for him because it was all just another dreadful blow to his pride. Francis was

[7]

out of work again for nearly a year before he struck upon the idea that what he really wanted to do was to write a history of suspension bridges.

As far as Francis knew there was no adequate book about suspension bridges. Of course there were books for specialists on the subject, but Francis had in mind a book which would be easily accessible to a lay public.

Claire was tremendously enthusiastic about the plan and did everything she could to encourage and help Francis. She ordered esoteric library books for him and collected them on her way back from work. She photocopied extracts from them for him and typed letters to engineering departments of universities. It was all wonderful; Francis had the flat to himself throughout the day with plenty of time for his researches and if he found it difficult to concentrate, he had only to go down the road to the local library and work there.

The more Francis thought about the matter, the harder he found it to decide exactly what he wanted to do. Perhaps he should broaden his subject to include cantilever bridges. Some of the finest bridges in the world were cantilever bridges.

Everywhere Francis went he talked about his project and the more he talked about it the more he realised that he would absolutely have to include a chapter on steel arch bridges since no work on bridges could possibly be complete without reference to the Adomi Bridge in Ghana in which high-strength friction-grip bolts were used at the connections between the chord members.

People nodded their heads wisely. Francis seemed to know a great deal about bridges and before long he would probably begin writing.

Nancy was thrilled for Claire's sake although George was more cautious than she in expressing his pleasure. He looked forward to hearing that the book had been begun and when it had he would look forward to hearing that it had been finished. As soon as it was finished then he would be as delighted as the rest of them, but in the meantime he would be glad to hear a little less talk and to see a little more action.

Six months went by without Francis putting pen to paper and some of his and Claire's friends began to be bored with hearing about Brunel and Roebling and the Howrah Bridge over the Hooghly River and the Oakland Bay Bridge and pile-cylinder foundations and box girders and cable anchorage.

The time had really come to start writing but whenever Claire suggested to Francis that he begin he seemed to suffer from an acute attack of asthma. She knew perfectly well that asthma attacks were frequently brought on by nerves and she understood that after talking about his project so much, Francis was probably nervous of writing and certainly frightened of not doing justice to both the subject and himself. She decided that the best thing to do was not to mention the book for a while. She still had faith in him and was perfectly certain that as soon as he began to write, his anxieties would fall away and he would be so happy with his work that it would come easily to him. She was sure that it would all be all right in the end but that Francis, who was a very sensitive person, should be left to do his work in his own time. Above all he must not be allowed to feel guilty. Guilt was a totally destructive force.

When Claire stopped mentioning the book, the asthma attacks grew less frequent and Francis himself began to talk less about bridges. Claire supposed that he was still thinking about them and she imagined that this quiet reflection would eventually lead to work. But gradually Francis stopped talking about bridges altogether and Claire was forced to the conclusion that he was not thinking about them either. She felt embarrassed for Francis and dreadfully sorry for him but she consoled herself by thinking that if he were capable of one idea and of so much enthusiasm for it, then he must surely be capable of another and that next time it might be a better idea. After all, how many people really wanted to read about bridges? The book would probably not have been a commercial

[9]

success and poor Francis's self-esteem would only have suffered another body blow. As it was, nothing had been lost.

After a while Francis got a job as a filing clerk in a solicitor's office. It was only a temporary job and it was also only the second job that he had had since leaving university. The job was, according to Francis, unbearably boring but Claire presumed that however boring, it must be good for his self-respect to be earning a little money.

Although their relationship was a sound one, Claire sometimes thought that Francis must suffer from living with somebody so much more successful than himself. Even these days a man's masculinity could be threatened if he compared himself to a more dynamic woman. In fact she had been confronted not only in her private life, but at work too, with the rather sad spectacle of the modern male – his supremacy at last threatened, perhaps even overthrown, a hesitant, questioning, worried creature, quite unsure of his new role.

Francis's temporary job came to an end at just about the time when Claire was due for a holiday and so she thought that they should go away together. Neither of them had ever been to Italy and a complete break would be good for them both. Sometimes Claire felt that life was so hectic that she and Francis did not have enough time for each other. They needed to talk things over and they needed to be away from their everyday surroundings and their usual crowd of friends. They even needed to be away from Nancy's baleful eye and George's studied determination not to interfere.

As for Francis's father – he presented no very real threat since he and Francis had fallen out some years ago and never saw each other any more. Francis's father did not harm Francis in the present, he had already done all the harm he could in the past – he and Francis's mother who had run away from home when her son was only a little boy, leaving him to be brought up by an overbearing, insensitive father.

Of course Claire knew that a mother's rejection was the ultimate rejection and this she must never forget if she occasionally felt annoyed with Francis for his weaknesses. Claire's own mother was sometimes tiresome. She had a rather old-fashioned approach to life and was even slightly prudish or so Claire thought, but it could never be suggested that she had not been a good and loving mother.

Sometimes Claire would glance at Francis and catch his delicate face in repose. His pale hooded eyes would have a far away look and then she would try to imagine him as a little boy at the age of about six when his mother left him. He must have been small for his age, pale and questioning even then with those large eyes and his usual serious expression. Or had the serious expression come as a result of the rejection? Poor Francis. It was hardly surprising that he had so little self-confidence. He had suffered the ultimate rejection. Whatever happened she, Claire, would make it up to him. She would stick by him forever, through thick and thin. She would teach him to believe in himself because he was worth believing in and eventually he would find a path for himself. It might not be bridges, but something would surely turn up.

Now, as she sat at her parents' table, Claire looked across at Francis who was politely listening to George expounding on the problems of our inner cities. Francis was so gentle and so polite – so agreeable that even George, against his better judgment, had grown quite fond of him – or at any rate used to him.

'Lovely lemon meringue,' said Claire, putting down her spoon and fork and turning to her mother. 'No one makes it better than you.'

'Have some more,' said Nancy. 'Your father and I will never eat it.'

Claire willingly had another helping but Francis preferred to light a cigarette if no one minded. Nancy never ceased to be amazed by the amount Francis smoked. You would hardly have thought that he could afford it since he was usually out of work. And it could hardly do his asthma any good.

While Claire finished her pudding Nancy got up to fetch the coffee, then George and Francis took their coffee into the sitting room while Claire helped her mother to wash up.

'Have you seen how lovely the dahlias are in my flowerbed this year?' said Nancy looking out of the window as she rinsed a plate.

'Lovely,' said Claire vaguely, and then, 'We talked things over very thoroughly while we were away. Francis is really determined to get down to doing something serious this autumn.'

'What sort of thing has he got in mind?' asked Nancy as she tied her flowered apron around her waist. 'I always use this apron you gave me.'

'Well, he's decided to take a course. You'd be surprised at the number of courses the community education service offers.'

'So what will he study?'

'He wants to do a course in something creative like jewellery-making or pottery. Probably jewellery-making because you need so much room for pottery and it will be something which he will develop at home after he's finished the course.

'In any case,' Claire went on, 'while we were in Italy we looked at a lot of jewellery. They make wonderful modern jewellery out there and Francis was quite inspired. I'm sure it's something he'd be really good at.'

When the washing up was finished, Nancy and Claire joined the men in the sitting room.

'It's a nice afternoon,' said Nancy, looking out of the window. 'Why don't we go for a short walk on the common? I'm sure we could all do with a breath of fresh air.' The room was heavy with tobacco smoke and Francis was just stubbing a cigarette out in an already full ashtray at his side.

'Come on Francis,' said Claire. 'You coming?'

Francis nodded and stood up.

George heaved himself out of his armchair, tapped out his pipe in the fireplace and glanced down at the dog lying peacefully at his feet.

'Come on old boy,' he said, 'walkies!'

CHAPTER II

Francis and Claire had made up their minds from the very start of their relationship that they would not get married until they were certain that they were sexually suited to each other. So many marriages these days ended in the divorce courts and they both felt that so long as they could be sure that they were well matched sexually their union would have an almost certain recipe for success.

Although they had now been living together for five years, Claire and Francis had not yet reached any firm conclusion as to their sexual compatibility. Of course at times it seemed as though they were all set to sail into marriage, and to live happily ever afterwards, but just as they were about to announce their engagement to the world something would happen to cast them both into a turmoil of doubt. For instance, Francis would get a cold.

Francis was one of those people who suffered from particularly heavy and often feverish colds – sometimes these colds would linger on for months, perhaps throughout the entire winter. Nobody suffering from such a cold could possibly be in peak sexual condition and so the decision would have to be postponed again.

At other times, perhaps as ill luck would have it, just when Francis had finally rid himself of a cold, Claire would be so exhausted from a heavy work load, or so concerned about some problem at work that she could hardly think about sex at all. This would leave Francis hurt and guilty because of what he saw as his inability to make Claire happy and so the problem would be perpetuated.

The holiday in Italy had been successful from every angle and they had returned burning with renewed lust for each other, optimistic that the situation might last and determined to give it until Christmas before making their final decision.

It was not as though Claire had any intention of leaving Francis in the event of their not getting married. On the contrary Claire certainly saw herself as permanently tied to Francis. He needed her and so long as he needed her she would stay by his side. To stay by his side was certainly no ordeal for Claire because she loved him and her greatest happiness was to care for him, to praise him, to stroke his brow, to hold his hand, to admire his beauty and to listen to his every problem.

Neither had Francis any intention of leaving Claire. In her, he claimed, he had found everything he could ever dream of in a woman. She was the mainstay of his life and with her – and her alone – he felt like a whole and valued person because she had persuaded him that she really cared and no one, no one else at all had ever really cared for him.

Claire and Francis lived in a small flat which was in fact the top floor of a Georgian terraced house in a London suburb. George and Nancy lived in the same suburb, about two miles away, in the 1930s mock-Elizabethan villa in which Claire and her brother, Roddy, had been brought up.

Ever since she was quite small Claire had instinctively known that she wanted to go into a 'caring' profession. For a long time she had wanted to be a nurse and so in those far off days she was permanently dressed in a nurse's uniform with a sick doll under her arm. Then one Christmas, when she was given a 'doctor's set', she became instantly and totally captivated by the little plastic stethoscope which was part of it and which she hung around her neck from that

[15]

day onwards until it finally perished or was lost. She hated to be parted from it and when she went to bed she used to keep it under her pillow to the consternation of Nancy who was convinced that one night she would strangle herself by mistake.

At about the same time that Claire was given her 'doctor's set' she learned to her delight that women as well as men could be doctors and so thrilled was she with the information that for many years after that she nurtured the hope that she would one day be a doctor.

Eventually, at about the time of her O-levels, Claire changed her mind. She no longer wanted to be a doctor, what she really wanted instead was to be a social worker.

Both George and Nancy were delighted by their daughter's decision. Claire was a warm-hearted, practical, hard-working girl, quite suited, in their opinion, to her chosen profession. Besides they were glad that she knew what she wanted to do and proud of her for wanting to do something worthwhile and of use to the community. They were at the time especially concerned about their son, Roddy, and were therefore all the more pleased by Claire's stability and sense of purpose.

After leaving school Claire took a degree in Sociology at London University and then went straight on for a year to the 'Tech' for her CQSW.

As soon as she qualified she was lucky to be employed by the County Council in her own area which pleased her as she did not really want to move away to another part of the country although during her training she had enjoyed placements in the Midlands and North of England. She settled quickly into the job and found that with one exception, the other members of her team were pleasant and easy to get on with. Her bearded team leader was a young man of about thirty-five whose seriousness, devotion to duty, understanding, energy and industry were a permanent source of inspiration to Claire. She enjoyed her job and the people she cared for, but she would do anything to prove her worth to her team leader.

Gradually Claire found that she became more and more involved with family problems and so when new family cases came up, they were as often as not handed over to her. Another young woman on the team usually took care of cases involving the elderly. So Claire loved her work and was soon a respected and much appreciated member of her team. It was after she had been working for a year that she met Francis. She met him at a party with some friends in London shortly after she had broken up with a young man with whom she had been going out for a year or two. She was instantly attracted to Francis, and he to her and within a very short time they set up house together.

On Monday, after lunching with her parents, Claire woke early. She and Francis had been back from Italy for just over a week and she had been back at work for a week. In a way she was glad to be back and eager to pick up where she had left off. There were families in her care for whom she felt tremendous concern and whom she did not like to abandon for too long. She was pleased at the prospect of seeing some of her families again and wondered how they had fared in her absence.

But, at the same time, she was worried about Francis. He had been so happy in Italy and now she hoped against hope that he would really be able to make something out of this jewellery thing.

Claire was up and making a pot of tea while Francis still lay in bed.

'D'you want some toast?' she called to him.

She didn't hear him answer so she put a slice of bread under the grill for him just the same. When the tea and the toast were made she went back to the bedroom.

'Come on,' she said. 'Breakfast's ready lazy bones.'

Francis stirred under the duvet. He hated getting up in the morning. As far as he could see you were either one of those people who liked the morning or you weren't. He certainly wasn't. It seemed to him that the best place to have breakfast was in bed and sometimes he managed to persuade Claire to bring his tea to him in bed but she usually made some silly excuse about it being impossible to eat or drink in bed, and once you had eaten a piece of toast in bed the crumbs seemed to be there forever.

In fact Claire had a sneaking feeling that if Francis was not out of bed by the time she left for work, he would still be there by the time she came back.

'Can't you bring me a cup of tea?' said Francis, catching hold of Claire's hand as she stood by the bed and glancing up at her with an appealing look.

Claire bent down to kiss him.

'Lazy bones!' she said. 'I can't go bringing you tea. I'm in a hurry to leave for work. And promise me you'll go down to the Tech today and sign on for that jewellery course.'

'Yes, yes, yes,' said Francis impatiently as he climbed unwillingly out of bed, wrapped a dressing gown around himself and followed Claire into the tiny kitchen.

'You've already left it for a whole week since getting back.'

'I was busy last week.'

'You must go today,' Claire went on. 'It would be dreadful if the course was full.'

'I've said I will,' said Francis, pouring out some tea.

'It's awfully exciting,' said Claire, changing her tack. 'I'm dying to see what you make.' She looked at her watch. 'Well, I must be off.' She tousled his hair, kissed his cheek, snatched up her bag and coat and was off.

As soon as he heard the flat door shut, Francis carried his mug of tea into the bedroom. He put it on the bedside table, went into the sitting room and picked up the television which he brought back into the bedroom and set down on a chair by the bed. He turned it on and climbed back into bed. Selina Scott was really quite pretty but he didn't much like what she was wearing. As for Frank Bough, Francis wondered what all the fuss was about. He supposed he was quite a nice fellow but he seemed a bit wet to him.

Francis stretched out his hand for his cigarettes from the bedside table. He took one out of the packet, lit it and then carefully counted how many remained.

[18]

Sod it! There were only nine, and nine would hardly last the morning out. He would have to go out and get some more at some stage. He gulped at his tea, glanced across at Frank Bough and vaguely began to plan his day. He thought he would probably go down to the Tech later on in the afternoon. He'd be more likely to find people about then. Not much point in going in the morning.

A ridiculous man in an enormous orange jersey which matched his hair had joined Frank and Selina and was talking about nerines, whatever they were. When he had finished boasting about his nerines and what a beautiful show they made in his garden, he began to talk about forcing bulbs for Christmas. Good God, could they never leave you alone? Some people had only just come back from their summer holiday and here they were already thrusting Christmas at you.

Suddenly Frank and Selina and the man in an orange jersey all faded away to be replaced by a newscaster who spoke of South Africa and Ulster and the Princess of Wales. Funny thing, really, the Princess of Wales looked quite like Selina Scott when you came to think about it. If he could get round to it Francis might find a picture of them both to send to *Private Eye* for their 'Look Alike' bit.

After the news Francis watched a repeat of Play School and then, when BBC1 went off the air he turned over to ITV.

By mid-morning he was beginning to run out of cigarettes and anyway the television was beginning to be boring so he started to think about getting up. About half an hour later he finally managed to heave himself out of bed. He ran his hand over his chin and decided that he wouldn't need to shave today and then remembered that he had promised Claire to go and sign on at the Tech. He didn't really feel like going down to the Tech and confronting some bossy secretary. He'd probably feel stronger after lunch. He pulled the duvet up over the bed, put the television back in the sitting room, and went to wash up his breakfast mug. One thing that sent Claire wild was to find the bed unmade and the breakfast all over the kitchen when she came in from work. Francis supposed that was fair enough. By noon he was in the Bricklayers Arms with a pint of beer in front of him and some cigarettes in his pocket. Things were looking up.

At about two o'clock Claire drove past the Bricklayers Arms on her way to visit a problem family in the area. She had had such a busy morning with a huge backlog of paperwork to get through that she had not had time to stop for lunch. She thought she might just pop into the pub for a sandwich or a packet of crisps, but on second thoughts, there was nowhere to park and it would only be a waste of time.

Inside Francis was still propping up the bar and telling the few regulars about this jewellery-making course which he was going to do. By the time the publican called for last orders Francis was feeling a bit fuzzy in the head. Stupid of him. He couldn't really go down to the Tech feeling like that so he decided to go to the cinema and sleep it off.

When he came out of the cinema he was feeling much better. He had seen about ten minutes of *A Hundred and One Dalmations* before dropping off to sleep. He was sorry to have fallen asleep in a way as the film looked quite good but the only trouble now, he realised as he looked at his watch, was that it was too late to go down to the Tech. There would hardly be anyone there as late as this in the afternoon. What a bloody bore! He had been looking forward to signing on to that jewellery-making course. Never mind, he could always do it the next day. He'd get up early in the morning and go down and sign on first thing. That's what he'd do. But he'd have to think of some excuse to give Claire who might really be quite cross with him. As he strolled back towards the flat he wondered what he would say to her. He hated letting Claire down because he loved her, so there was no question of telling her that he just hadn't got up in time, that he had had too much to drink at lunchtime and then gone to sleep in the cinema. He could imagine the hurt, disappointed look on her face if he told her the truth. No, he would have to think up something better than that. For a moment he felt slightly ashamed of himself. He really must make some sort of an effort to put some order into his life – if only for Claire's sake. He would love her to be proud of him. Perhaps jewellery-making was not really his thing and he ought to think of something else – but what? A sudden surge of panic welled up inside him and beads of sweat broke out on his forehead. As he tried to take a deep breath he felt the familiar congestion in his chest and delved frantically in his pocket for his ventilator.

He stopped walking and leaned against a lamp-post, waiting for the attack to subside, which with the aid of the ventilator it soon did.

As Francis walked up the street towards the house in which he lived, who should he see walking towards him and gesticulating madly, but Claire's brother, Roddy. That was a bit of luck! Francis had no time for Roddy, but if he told Claire that Roddy had turned up and prevented him from going down to the Tech she would believe him. He would just say that Roddy had appeared at the beginning of the afternoon. Roddy would willingly back up the lie and then Francis would go to the Tech first thing in the morning and everything would be all right. What a stroke of luck.

'Hullo there, Roddy, nice to see you. Come on up.' Francis put his front-door key in the lock.

'Do you mind if I do?' said Roddy. 'I'd like a word with you. Is Claire in?'

'No, she's not likely to be back from work till about half-six,' said Francis as they climbed the stairs. 'Do you mind saying when she comes in that you've been here all afternoon? It's just that I said I'd do something I haven't done – nothing much – but it might make it easier.'

'No problem,' said Roddy with a wink.

They reached the top of the stairs and Francis opened the door of the flat.

'Come on in,' he said.

[21]

'You been up to no good?' Roddy asked. 'Two-timing my little sister, you bugger.' He winked again and nudged Francis so hard in the ribs with his elbow that Francis nearly lost his balance.

'No, nothing like that,' said Francis coldly.

'Got anything to drink in this place?' Roddy asked as he flung himself down on the sofa, spreading his legs out in front of him.

Francis was beginning to wonder if the advantages of Roddy's arrival were not outweighed by the disadvantages.

'I think there are a couple of cans of beer in the fridge,' he said. 'And we may even have a drop of whisky.' He looked at his watch. 'It's no good going down to the pub yet – it won't be open.' He looked in a cupboard and brought out a bottle of whisky. It was three quarters full.

'That'll do fine,' said Roddy. 'I'll have it on the rocks.'

Francis went to the kitchen to fetch some glasses and the ice. Claire wouldn't be at all pleased to find him and her brother boozing when she got home, but it wasn't his fault if Roddy turned up unexpectedly. He could hardly turn him away. He poured the drinks and sat down on a chair opposite Roddy. He wished Roddy would shave off that ridiculous moustache. Young men looked horrible with moustaches. It crossed his mind that even without his moustache Roddy would look pretty horrible. He tried to remember if that moustache had been there when he first met Roddy. He thought it had. He fingered his own stubble. It was getting quite long. He'd probably have to shave again tomorrow but he might just get away with leaving it until Wednesday.

'Spot of trouble,' said Roddy. 'Any chance I could touch you for fifty quid? I can let you have it back next week without fail.'

Francis thought that Roddy must know someone who was not on the dole from whom he could borrow fifty pounds. He himself was certainly in no position to lend anyone five pounds – let alone fifty. He had lent small sums to Roddy in the past but had never been paid back so even if he'd had fifty pounds he wouldn't have been too keen to give it to Roddy.

'I think you owe me a tenner,' said Francis, 'do you remember about a fortnight before we went to Italy . . . ?'

'Now look here, I don't want to hear another word about that,' Roddy cut Francis short, 'but if you had fifty quid, you could help me out of a spot of bother. You'll get it back by next week without fail.'

'I'm afraid that I just don't have fifty pounds,' said Francis. 'If I gave you a cheque it would bounce.' He felt in his pocket for his wallet. 'I can lend you a fiver,' he said, 'but that's about it.' He held out a five pound note.

'A fiver's no good to me,' said Roddy, as he leaned towards Francis and took the crumpled note. 'I need fifty. Can't you get it off Claire? She earns a good living.'

'You'll have to ask her when she gets in.' As he spoke Francis realised that he would have to get some money off Claire himself in the morning or he wouldn't be able to buy any cigarettes. That fiver was supposed to last him for another couple of days until his dole cheque came in.

When Claire came back at half past six she was not at all pleased to find her brother ensconced in the sitting room, drinking whisky with Francis. God only knew how long he had been there. They had probably both had too much to drink by now and she was exhausted. She had had nothing to eat since breakfast and she had spent the whole afternoon visiting a couple of particularly problematic families. She was hungry and felt emotionally drained. Roddy's presence probably meant that he wanted to borrow some money.

Roddy jumped to his feet and planted a wet kiss on Claire's cheek.

'Good to see you Claire old girl,' he said. 'Sit down and have a whisky.'

'I'm starving,' said Claire and disappeared into the kitchen to find something to eat. She cut herself some bread and cheese and made herself some coffee which she brought back to the sitting room.

[23]

'So what can I do for you?' she asked as she sat down next to Roddy.

'Sixty quid,' said Roddy. 'Fifty-five – sixty quid would do nicely to get me out of a spot of bother. You'll get it back by next week without fail.'

CHAPTER III

Nancy had only a few memories of life before the war and those that she had were dim and mostly of apparently unconnected events and things. She remembered the huge clump of pampas grass in the corner of the garden of the house near Duxford in Cambridgeshire. She remembered the pink blancmange which came out of a rabbit shaped mould and which used to be served for lunch on Sundays and she remembered leaving her favourite doll outside all night to be found ruined and soaked by rain in the morning. She had a vague memory of walks along the village street, of a blue smocked dress and of a very fat lady in a hairnet and flowered overall who used to come in to help her mother with the housework.

She could hardly remember her father at all and those memories which she did have she confused in her imagination with the photographs of a handsome airman in battledress which stood on her mother's bedside table and which she later grew to know so well. She could remember him holding her 'fairy cycle' as she pedalled furiously, determined to learn to ride it all alone, and she could remember him bouncing her up and down on his knee as he chanted, 'This is the way the ladies ride' and , 'This is the way the farmers ride . . .' In all her memories of him he had a forage cap perched jauntily on the side of his head and was wearing battledress. She supposed when she thought about it later that she must sometimes have seen him dressed differently but she could never imagine how.

When Nancy was seven her father's plane was shot down over the Thames Estuary during the Battle of Britain and he was killed. She remembered being told that he was among those who would never come back and she remembered very acutely a feeling of immense pride in the knowledge that her father was a hero. This feeling of pride was far more intense than any sense of loss as she gazed in wonder at her mother's pale, silent face and tried to divine the secrets of her adult heart. But as well as pride she was conscious of a strong sense of guilt that she did not feel more unhappy but, rather, vaguely excited.

Shortly after her father died – Nancy never really knew how long – she and her mother moved away from the house near Duxford to live with Nancy's maternal grandmother in Bromley, Kent, and there she lived until she was grown-up, in fact until she married George in her early twenties.

Nancy's grandmother was a widow who lived in a pre-war villa which was kept in a permanent state of the utmost neatness. Mrs Larders ruled her house with a rod of iron. In return for providing her daughter and grand-daughter with a home she expected them entirely to relinquish their privacy and not a detail of their uneventful lives did she imagine could be kept from her. She seemed oblivious of the fact that the more uneventful a person's life is, the greater his need for secrecy. To a certain extent Nancy's mother, who, in order to make both ends meet, took a job as a receptionist for a local dentist and whose whole emotional self was taken up with reminiscence and hero worship of her late husband, was able to cope with Mrs Larders's interference. But Nancy found her childhood and girlhood stifling.

One of the worst aspects of life in the villa in Bromley was Nancy's mother's morbid interest in her late husband. On her bedside table she set up a kind of altar to his memory. There, on a lace mat, she placed three large photographs of him. In one he was standing, his hands behind his back, his legs apart, laughing in a garden; in another he sat astride a motorbike, smiling at the camera; the third was a head and shoulders portrait – probably an enlarged polyphoto – in which once again, he was laughing. In all three pictures the Squadron Leader was in battledress, and in front of them, throughout the seasons of the year, his widow arranged little bouquets of flowers. On either side of the pictures were birthday cake candles in little brass candle sticks. Whenever Nancy was thought by her mother to have misbehaved she was brought to the altar.

'What do you suppose your poor father in heaven who died for his country would think?' Nancy's mother would ask. And Nancy would hang her head in shame.

'Say you're sorry to Daddy,' her mother would order.

Nancy would apologise and then she would have to kiss the three photographs of the smiling airman, just as she had to kiss them every night when she said goodnight to her father.

On one such occasion when Nancy was about twelve she had the impression that her father winked at her. First the laughing airman in the garden winked and then the handsome airman on the motorbike winked and lastly the smiling airman in the polyphoto winked. The more Nancy thought about it the more certain she became that he had winked at her and so from that time onwards her visits to her father's shrine took on a new significance. She no longer dreaded them as she had done before, but looked forward to them as magical moments of connivance – times when she could share a secret with her father – a secret from which her mother and grandmother were completely excluded.

As Nancy grew older her emotional attachment to the man in the pictures developed and altered. She began to hope that one day she would meet such a handsome, blond young man with so debonair a smile. She imagined him kissing her in a rosy arbour and she imagined him on one knee in front of her, swearing eternal love. Very occasionally, late at night, she imagined other things. But in the morning she was ashamed of what she had thought and put such impure things out of her mind.

Nancy went to school at a local Roman Catholic convent. No one in her family had ever been a Catholic so far as she knew and, until she went to the convent, she had little if any understanding of Catholicism. She went there because her mother wanted her to go to a private school and the fees at the convent were low. For this reason, she was not by any means the only Protestant at the school.

For the most part the Protestant girls stuck together and although Nancy's semi-Catholic upbringing may have accentuated in her an awareness of 'wrong' she never bothered to adopt Catholicism, nor did she ever seriously consider doing so, but rather pitied the Catholic girls for having to fast on Fridays and to go into retreat during the Easter term.

Like most girls of her age she took a secretarial course on leaving school and by the time she was nineteen she was gainfully employed as a secretary with a local insurance firm.

Nancy had very little social life at this time which was during the early Fifties. Her grandmother, who was old and somewhat bad-tempered, and her mother, who was still preoccupied with the Squadron Leader, had few friends. Neither of them went out much, except in the case of Nancy's mother to work – and they rarely invited people in. Nancy had a few school friends with whom she would go to the cinema on Saturday evenings or for walks on the common on Sundays. Sometimes they invited her to their houses but she was reluctant to go as she feared she could not return their hospitality.

The retired Major who lived in the house next door to Nancy used to watch from his window as she walked to work.

'Pretty girl that Nancy,' he used to say to his wife, 'but if you ask me what she needs is a good roll in the hay.'

The major's wife looked suitably disapproving.

[28]

Nancy herself would probably have agreed with the major, but for the time being her romantic life was restricted to daydreaming about Frank Sinatra or Stewart Granger or to lengthy fantasising about her glamorous airman. In her bedroom she had a gramophone and she would lie on her bed at weekends and in the evenings, listening over and over again to the record of *South Pacific* which was enjoying a tremendous success at Drury Lane at the time. She had to play her gramophone very quietly in order not to disturb her grandmother who deplored what she described as frivolous modern nonsense. In those days Nancy was a quiet, dreamy, somewhat introverted person, but she was not really unhappy as she felt quietly confident that some enchanted evening she too would see a stranger across a crowded room. A blond, smiling stranger with a forage cap perched jauntily on the side of his head and wearing battledress. He would see her and wink . . .

It was not like that at all when Nancy met Gregory.

Mr Matravers, Nancy's boss, was showing Gregory around the office.

'This is Mr Finch,' said Mr Matravers. 'He will be joining us on Monday.'

Mr Finch stood awkwardly beside Mr Matravers, twisting a soft brown hat in his rather coarse hands. His short hair was neatly parted and he was wearing a grey suit. He was neither good-looking nor ugly, neither tall nor short, neither dark nor fair. He looked nervous and pleasant and ordinary and yet as Nancy glanced up something about him struck her with extraordinary force. She would never go so far as to say that she had fallen in love with him there and then as he stood awkwardly twisting his soft brown hat in his hands but she was aware of a strange acuteness in the moment. Later she would always remember the vividness of that moment as clearly as she remembered any other moment in her life.

On the Friday of Gregory's first week at work he hesitantly approached Nancy to ask her what she was doing on Saturday, for he had noticed Nancy just as she had noticed him but with his customary shyness he had not dared to address a word to her during the week, apart from a polite 'Good morning' and 'Good-bye' spoken with downcast eyes.

Nancy had no plans for Saturday and so, emboldened by the sweetness of her smile and the frankness of her gaze, Gregory suggested that she might meet him for tea in Fuller's tea rooms. If there was anything good on at the cinema perhaps she would like to go with him.

When Nancy set out to meet Gregory on Saturday afternoon she told her grandmother that she was going to meet an old school friend. There was no particular need for the lie except that she felt a desperate need for a private life. Why should she share everything with her grandmother and why should she – now nearly twenty years old – have to put up with the endless, prurient questioning to which her grandmother would submit her? Besides Nancy somehow felt that to discuss Gregory at home would be to diminish him. It did not occur to her that she was in love with him although she felt that since she first set eyes on him, twisting his soft brown hat so awkwardly in his hands, there had been an indefinable excitement in the air.

After walnut cake and tea at Fuller's, Nancy and Gregory went to the cinema. In those good old days, the seats only cost two shillings and ninepence each. When they came out of the cinema Gregory offered to walk Nancy home but as they reached the end of the road in which she lived she had to leave him.

'I'm afraid I told my mother that I'd gone out with an old school friend,' Nancy was forced to explain and she blushed as she did so.

Gregory was somehow flattered to discover that he had been lied about and laughed as he said good-bye.

After that Gregory and Nancy began to see each other regularly. In the office they hardly spoke to each other but walnut cake at Fuller's followed by the cinema became a feature of Saturday afternoons. On Sundays they used to meet for long walks when they would talk and talk and talk, telling each other every detail of their lives and holding hands as they walked.

They seemed to have a great deal in common as both were only children and both lived with a widowed mother.

Gregory's mother suffered acutely from the appalling condition known as agoraphobia. He had not been properly aware of it during his school days at the local boys' grammar school after which he had been called up. He spent most of his military service stationed in Germany and it was not until he returned from there a couple of months earlier that he realised quite the gravity of his mother's condition. She had now reached the point where she could never ever leave the house. It was lucky that Gregory lived at home and could look after her and do the shopping.

Because of their peculiar family circumstances Gregory and Nancy never invited each other home. There seemed to be an unspoken agreement on the subject between them, besides which they both had every good reason to wish to escape from the claustrophobic atmosphere of their own houses.

Nancy and Gregory fell more and more in love as the weeks went by. The world seemed bathed in golden light, everyday life took on a new and glorious intensity, spring was in the air and hope was in their hearts.

Mrs Larders was no fool. She told her daughter that she ought to be keeping a close eye on Nancy. If Mrs Larders wasn't mistaken Nancy was up to something. Was she really meeting school friends every weekend? You couldn't trust young people these days. Now it was quite a different matter when Mrs Larders was young.

The Major in the house next door remarked to his wife as he watched Nancy from his window that that Nancy grew prettier every day. Must be in love or something, she was always singing as she went to work.

It was partly the singing which had aroused Mrs Larders's suspicions. What was there for the child to sing about? She was always singing. Singing in the bath, singing on the stairs, singing in the kitchen, singing when she came home from work. It quite got on Mrs Larders's nerves, all that silly singing.

Nancy began to long for the day when Gregory would propose to her. She realised that as he was not very well-off he might feel that he could not afford to marry yet, but she didn't mind waiting and as she waited she daydreamed about the home in which they would live together. Alone in her bedroom at night Nancy no longer thought about the handsome airman. His face had vanished from her fantasies for ever, to be replaced by Gregory's. But her mother still insisted that she say goodnight to her father every evening before she went to bed. This routine had lost its horror and its magic at last and Nancy performed it automatically to please her mother whom she regarded as vaguely dotty.

One day when Mrs Larders was out shopping a neighbour told her that she had seen Nancy at the cinema on Saturday with a nice young man. Mrs Larders was incensed. The dirty, deceitful little hussy! Mrs Larders would soon deal with her. How dared the child be so sly.

That evening after work Nancy came singing her way up the garden path only to be greeted at the front door by her grandmother with a face of thunder.

'I want a word with you young woman,' said Mrs Larders sharply. She gripped her grand-daughter firmly by the upper arm and pushed her into the sitting room.

Nancy immediately realised what was up.

Mrs Larders wanted to know how long this had been going on.

Nancy lied. She said that last Saturday was the first time that she had gone out with Gregory. He worked in her office and was a very nice boy. She couldn't think why she had lied. It just seemed simpler at the time and she was extremely sorry.

Mrs Larders didn't believe a word. She didn't like liars and she didn't like sluts. Where else had they been together and what had they done? Did he touch her? Did he hold her hand? Had he kissed her?

[32]

So he hadn't kissed her! Mrs Larders didn't believe that either. She knew men. How had he kissed her? Where had he kissed her? When had he kissed her and how often and where had he put his hands when he kissed her?

Nancy looked at her grandmother for the first time with utter contempt and loathing. She wanted to be sick. How dared this vile woman talk to her in this way? She was trying to make Nancy feel guilty for her innocent happiness.

'Don't you know,' screamed Mrs Larders at fever pitch, 'that men only want one thing? If you once lead them on they can't be stopped. They're not like women, they have no self-control. They're like wild animals . . .'

Nancy glanced coldly at her grandmother standing there howling in front of her – rather like a wild animal herself – then she turned on her heel and left the room. She went upstairs to her bedroom and shut and locked the door. She refused to come down to supper that night, saying that she had a headache and was not hungry. For the first time in her life Nancy felt that she had stood up, however feebly, to her grandmother, and neither had she, for the first time since she could remember, said goodnight to her father.

For the next two weeks Mrs Larders forbade Nancy to leave the house at the weekends. Nancy had no option but to obey although it struck her as perfectly ridiculous that at the age of very nearly twenty she should be allowed so little freedom.

But Mrs Larders was not so clever as she thought. By the third week she said that Nancy could go out with a girlfriend provided the girlfriend came to the house to meet her so that Mrs Larders could be sure that everything was above board. In fact she was beginning to be rather irritated by seeing the girl hanging around the house and moping thoughout Saturday and Sunday.

Nancy lost no time in fixing up a girlfriend as a cover and so by Saturday afternoon she was once again free. She had had a few whispered exchanges with Gregory in the office and so he knew what had happened, but she longed to be able to speak to him again properly and alone. That Saturday afternoon instead of going to Fuller's and to the cinema they went to the common. They walked and walked and talked and talked. They both had so much to say to each other and they were worried by Mrs Larders's ability to interfere with their relationship.

As dusk began to fall they sat down together on the grass, still totally engrossed in each other and it was then that Gregory told Nancy how much he loved her and how he had missed talking to her for the past two weeks. He wanted to marry her but could not begin to afford to yet. Would she be prepared to wait a year or two for him? Of course she would. She would wait for eternity. Then as the darkness thickened they made love.

The following day was Sunday and the same thing happened again. By Monday Nancy began to worry that perhaps she had really been too imprudent. Supposing she were pregnant? But somehow the idea seemed ridiculous and anyway she was so elated that even if she were pregnant she felt that it wouldn't matter. So she sang her way through the week, walking on air as she did so, and looking forward to the following weekend.

When Saturday came again Gregory said that he did not want to go to the common. The weather was not very nice and he took her to tea in Fuller's. As they sat in a quiet corner waiting for their tea and walnut cake Nancy began to wonder if something were wrong. Gregory was very quiet.

Eventually Gregory began to talk, quietly and with an occasional catch in his voice. Since last weekend he had been suffering the most appalling pangs of guilt. He had betrayed Nancy's confidence and taken advantage of her. He was deeply ashamed of himself. He ought, if he were half a man, to marry Nancy immediately but for one thing her mother would probably not give her permission and for another Gregory could honestly not afford to marry. There was a third consideration, and that was Gregory's mother.

As for Nancy, she could see no need for guilt. What had happened was as much her fault as his and she had no regrets. She had told Gregory that she would wait for him until eternity and nothing had changed that.

But Gregory went on. Nancy probably did not realise quite what a problem his mother was. She had no one in the world to look after her but him and it would be quite impossible to ask anybody to share the burden with him. So long as he had to care for his mother he would be in no position to marry. He could not do anything so selfish. Gregory was tortured by guilt whichever way he looked at the situation but he had decided that his relationship with Nancy must end, a decision which it broke his heart to make, and all that was left was for him to beg her forgiveness.

Nancy didn't eat her walnut cake that day and on the following Monday she took immediate steps to change her job. She stopped singing in the bathroom and on the stairs and in the kitchen, she stopped putting her hair in curlers at night and she walked with a heavy tread.

The Major in the house next door said to his wife,

'Young Nancy's not looking as pretty as she was, these days.'

For a long time Nancy refused even to go to the cinema with her girlfriends at weekends. The light had gone out of her life and there was no hope.

Mrs Larders was glad to see that the child appeared to have come to her senses.

CHAPTER IV

Claire thought, as she drank her tea alone in the kitchen, that it was time that somebody gave Roddy a talking to. But she wondered if there was anybody to whom he would listen. Of course he had not returned the fifty pounds which she had lent him ten days ago – not that she had ever really expected him to do so. One day she would just have to be strong and refuse to lend him any more money. In any case she was not particularly well off and wasn't really in a position to keep handing money out to her brother. She knew that she only did it for her parents' sake and she suspected that Roddy knew that too, so he was exerting some kind of moral blackmail over her. Claire was terrified of what would happen if she refused to give Roddy money. He might do anything and it would break her parents' hearts if he ever got into trouble with the police.

That night – at about two or three o'clock in the morning – Claire had been woken by the telephone. Of course it was Roddy – this time asking Claire to give him an alibi. Claire didn't like the idea of that at all. It would hardly do for someone with her job to be caught lying to the police. Even if she weren't a social worker, she wouldn't be the sort of person to give false evidence.

'Oh come on Claire, don't be so bloody pompous, you little nit wit.' Roddy had sounded quite nasty. 'You always were a goody-goody. All I'm asking is for you to tell a tiny fib to get your only brother out of a spot of bother.'

It was the middle of the night and Claire's mind felt blurred by sleep. All she wanted was to get back to bed.

'Well,' she said reluctantly, 'as long as it's nothing to do with the police.'

'Now listen here, why would Roddy be involved with the police? Just why? Of course it's nothing to do with the police. Just a spot of trouble with a woman.' Roddy laughed a vulgar laugh. 'Well, that's agreed then. I knew you wouldn't let your big brother down. If anyone asks you, I spent all night at your place. But remember, not a word to Mum and Dad.' Without so much as a 'good-bye', Roddy was gone.

Claire stumbled back to bed only to find that Francis had taken most of the duvet. She pulled at it angrily, not caring if she woke him. If she were a different type of person she felt she might burst into tears. What was the matter with the men in her life? Why did she always have to be the strong one? And Francis still hadn't been and signed on at the Tech. She was beginning to doubt that he ever would. But there must be something he would like to do even if it weren't jewellery making. She wondered what.

In the morning Claire was still feeling angry and Francis continued to sleep deeply as she dressed. She wondered what on earth made him so tired that he could sleep soundly all night and still sleep through the alarm clock in the morning. She had lain awake for some time after Roddy's telephone call which didn't appear to have woken Francis either. What the hell was wrong with everyone?

She stamped into the kitchen and made herself a cup of tea and a piece of toast without bothering to call Francis. When she had finished her breakfast she crept out of the flat as quietly as she could and pulled the door shut gently behind her.

There was not really all that much point in trying to be so quiet, she could have clattered around the flat for hours and slammed the front door without there being any danger of Francis stirring.

[37]

Once she was in the street Claire felt a faint pang of conscience. Poor Francis, she had never left for work before without saying good-bye to him, or making him a cup of tea. She very nearly turned round and went back up to the flat but she glanced at her watch and realised that if she did she would be late for work. Anyway, she thought, as she turned the ignition of her emerald green Deux Chevaux, perhaps I am killing him by kindness and I ought to be tougher with him. Perhaps a shock would do him good. As she drove away to work it struck Claire – not for the first time – that she was far more clear sighted when it came to the immense and appalling problems of some of the families in her care than she ever was over her own comparatively minor ones.

When Claire reached her office she found Barry, her bearded team leader, was already at work. He looked up and smiled in his usual friendly way as she came through the door. Claire loved Francis but sometimes she could wish that he were just a little bit more like Barry – Barry who was always so clean and spruce and punctual and energetic and positive and good humoured. She gave him an exceptionally warm smile in return.

'Well Claire, I think we've got one for you this morning – no, I wouldn't bother to take off your coat. I think you ought to pop round straight away to this address.' Barry handed Claire a piece of paper.

There had been three separate calls in the last half hour from people suspecting a severe case of child beating. One had come from a neighbour who was too frightened to give her name and another from a man who hadn't identified himself in any way. The third call had come from an infant teacher who was beginning to be suspicious about a child in her class who often appeared to have strange bruises on her body and who was also frequently absent from school. She had not been in for the last few days.

The school teacher had been able to give a rough account of the family background. It was pretty much the usual sort of story – out-of-work father – and there was some uncertainty as to whether or not he was in fact married to the mother who was very young and had several small children.

As Claire got back into her little green car she wondered what would come of the visit. It sounded to her like the sort of case where she might have trouble in gaining access. She drove straight to Thackeray Buildings, a gloomy block of council flats which she knew well and parked in front of them.

The flats, along with the Dickens and Trollope and Brontë Buildings, were some thirty years old, about four storeys high and built in the most depressing style imaginable, of purplish red brick, with tiny windows and outside staircases.

Claire always thought that that particular purple brick looked feverish and diseased. She could well imagine resorting to despair for no other reason than that one lived in Thackeray or Dickens or Brontë Buildings. It made her quite angry to think of Roddy's comfortable, privileged upbringing and what he'd made of it. Where, she vaguely wondered, had her mother gone wrong? Her poor mother.

She climbed the outside staircase to number thirty-eight on the third floor, and knocked on the door. From indoors there came the sound of a baby crying and a woman's voice said, 'Belt up, will yer?'

After a pause Claire knocked again – there was no bell.

The door of the next door flat opened and a woman's head appeared. At the level of the woman's thigh, the head of a small child appeared. Both stared balefully at Claire before disappearing, and then the door was shut again.

The volume of crying inside number thirty-eight increased, then a door slammed and Claire heard footsteps approaching.

Her first reaction to the sight of the immensely fat young woman with an infinitely expressionless face who opened the door was one of pity. The woman's short, light brown hair lay in greasy strands against her head. She was dressed in a black miniskirt, a pink jersey and turquoise bedroom slippers. Her thighs were so painfully fat that she seemed to stand with her feet unnaturally far apart. Her legs, on which she wore neither tights nor stockings, but a pair of yellow ankle socks, looked blotchy and uncomfortable. She could not have been more than twenty-one or twenty-two years old.

'Mrs Flack?' Claire asked. The fat woman nodded. Claire explained who she was and said that she had heard from the school that Yolande had been away quite a lot and she had just called to see if the family needed any help or advice.

Mrs Flack half closed the door.

'We don't need no help, we're all right,' she said.

'Is Yolande at home today?' Claire asked. 'I'd like to say hello to her if she is.'

Mrs Flack grudgingly opened the door again.

'Oh, all right then, seeing as you're here you might as well come in.'

Claire stepped through the door into a passage which seemed to smell all at once of frying and stale cigarettes and wet nappies. A push-chair and a small tricycle almost entirely blocked the entrance. The noise of crying children which came from behind a closed door at the end of the passage reached a crescendo. Next to that door was another half open door which, judging from Claire's knowledge of the layout of the flats, must be the kitchen.

To Claire's left was another closed door. Mrs Flack opened it and said,

'Come in the front room.'

The front room was small and narrow. Two of the walls were covered with huge grubby lime green poppies, and the other two walls were painted a pale shade of mauve. The woodwork, like the poppies, was lime green and the paint was chipped in many places. The room had clearly not been redecorated for some time.

Mrs Flack pointed to a chair and invited Claire to sit down. She sat down opposite her.

'I'll go along in a minute and see if Yolande's awake,' she

[40]

said. 'She was a bit off-colour this morning which is why I didn't send her to school.'

Claire glanced around the poorly furnished room and down at the thread-bare carpet which was covered with crumbs and what looked like dog hairs. As if to confirm Claire's suspicions, there was a scratch at the door.

'It must be the bleedin' dog,' said Mrs Flack as she levered her huge body off the settee and lumbered towards the door which she opened to let in an enormous Old English Sheepdog.

'This is Barry,' she said. 'We calls 'im after Barry Manilow.'

Claire couldn't help thinking of Barry, her wonderful, spruce, energetic team leader and neither could she help remarking that Barry must eat quite a lot.

'E's probably been helpin' hisself to somefink as 'e didn' ought to in the kitchen while I was talkin' to you,' said Mrs Flack. She turned to the dog. 'Bleedin' nuisance you are,' she said and cuffed it over the head. Then she sank down on the settee again and Barry spread himself out at her feet, taking up what seemed to be most of the room.

'Well,' said Claire briskly, 'as I'm here, perhaps you wouldn't mind my asking you a few questions. We'd like to be sure that you're receiving all the help to which you are entitled, depending on your family circumstances.'

Despite her expressionless face and flat voice Mrs Flack seemed remarkably willing to talk and was surprisingly articulate. Poor thing, thought Claire, she's obviously lonely and depressed and probably relieved to find anyone to talk to after being shut up in here with those crying babies.

Claire looked sympathetic and kind. Mrs Flack didn't mind her although her instinct was to mistrust those prying people from the Welfare.

Yolande was Mrs Flack's eldest child. She was going on six, was Yolande. Mrs Flack was fifteen when Yolande was born. It was a bit of bad luck her getting pregnant like that – she only went with Gary twice before she was pregnant and

[41]

lots of girls she knew had been going with boys for years without getting pregnant. It was just her luck.

Mrs Flack's mother, who sounded to Claire like a very determined woman, had stopped her daughter from having an abortion – in any case it would probably have been too late by the time she found out about the pregnancy – and had arranged for her to marry Gary as soon as she was sixteen. Gary was a couple of years older.

The couple were at first reasonably happily married. Mrs Flack was soon pregnant again and the young family moved into a council flat. There followed two miscarriages before Trevor and finally Dana were born. Gary had been unemployed now for over two years. Nowadays he came home less and less often and usually only for somewhere to sleep. Mrs Flack suspected him of messing around with other girls. It wasn't fair was it? It was always the women what suffered.

Claire had heard it all before with the only difference that as often as not the young women were not married and their children had different fathers. But, by and large, she was inclined to agree with Mrs Flack that it was the women what suffered, although she didn't bother to add that Gary Flack might not feel too happy at having been pushed into a teenage marriage and at finding himself, aged twenty-two or three, unemployed, the father of a large family and the husband of a depressed young woman whose physical appearance might well make him recoil. She felt sorry for Gary and sorry for his wife just as she always felt sorry when she heard the appalling details of other people's misfortunes.

And then there was the dog which must eat as much as all the children put together. Claire was puzzled by that enormous dog.

When Mrs Flack had finally stopped talking, she heaved herself out of her seat again and said that she would go and see if the children were awake.

Claire rose to her feet too, and suggested coming with her. Mrs Flack hesitated before saying,

'This way then.'

Barry, the dog, stood up, shook itself and followed Mrs Flack into the passage. Claire followed the dog. The sound of children crying had not stopped from the moment Claire entered the flat.

When the small procession reached the children's door Mrs Flack opened it and went in but as Claire prepared to follow, the dog blocked the doorway, turned, lowered its head between its huge shoulders and began to growl ferociously.

Claire backed swiftly into the passage.

'Our Barry don't never let no one come in the kids' room,' said Mrs Flack by way of explanation from the other side of the door.

Claire wasn't quite sure what to do. This was a new one on her. She wondered frantically what Barry, her team leader, would do under the same circumstances. Having got this far she would feel an awful fool if she went back to the office unable to report on the child, Yolande Flack. After all, no fewer than three people had telephoned to express their concern about the little girl.

'Hello Yolande,' she called feebly through the door.

Barry, the dog, growled more threateningly than ever.

'Say hello to the lady, Yolande,' Mrs Flack's voice came from inside the room. Her remark was followed by a long wail.

A thin, grubby little boy with his thumb in his mouth and mucus from a runny nose smeared all over his face, appeared at the door. He was wearing nothing but nappies which came half way down his legs, and rubber pants.

'Get back in bed Trevor,' yelled Mrs Flack. 'Yer'll catch yer bleedin' def.'

The little boy patted the dog nonchalantly on the back and disappeared into the bedroom.

'Perhaps you could bring Yolande out to see me,' Claire suggested, 'and Dana too.'

'She's got a cold 'ant she, and I don't want her to catch 'er def,' said Mrs Flack. 'I'll just let 'er look out the door.'

[43]

For an instant Mrs Flack appeared with a barely visible, wailing child wrapped in a dirty blanket. Then Claire heard her say,

'Get back in bed and belt up will yer.' A few moments later she appeared with another much smaller bundle.

'And this 'ere's our Dana,' she said.

Claire took a step forward in the hope of getting a better view of the child so as to be able to form some opinion of its physical condition but as soon as she moved, the dog moved too, thrusting its great shaggy head towards Claire and snarling.

After Mrs Flack had put the second bundle back where it belonged, she came out of the room, pushed the dog into it and shut the door.

'Won't he hurt the children?' Claire asked anxiously.

'Naar,' said Mrs Flack. 'If 'e do I'll thrash the 'ide off 'im.'

Claire felt somewhat defeated. She had not had what could in any way be described as an adequate look at the child. In fact she was acutely aware that of all the children, Yolande was the one which she had been least able to assess. The little boy had looked dirty and becolded, no worse – but she would not care to make any judgment concerning the physical well-being of either of the girls. She would call again soon at a different time of day. Perhaps the children would be out of their room and she would have a better chance of seeing them. She felt she could do no more for the moment.

As Mrs Flack opened the front door to let Claire out a renewed wave of wailing arose from the room at the end of the corridor.

Claire sighed as the door closed behind her, and she began to hurry down the outside staircase. She had a feeling that Mrs Flack and all the little Flacks were going to be with her for some time to come. Poor woman, she thought. And only twenty-one. Then she felt that old familiar twinge of guilt which recurred whenever she compared her own good fortune to the miserable lives of the people she met through her work.

[44]

As she crossed the road and walked towards her car she noticed that a grey minivan with a ladder on its roof had parked so tightly in front of her that she would have some difficulty in getting out. Just as she was unlocking the door of her car, a young man got out of the minivan. He turned towards her with a wide smile and said,

'Sorry Miss, I don't seem to have left you much room.'

'I expect I can manage,' said Claire, smiling back and getting into her car. 'It's not your fault – it's almost impossible to find anywhere to park around here – '

'Blame Maggie for that,' said the young man, grinning. 'Mrs Fatcher's Britain – what a Paradise!' He laughed and began to direct Claire so as to help her out. 'Woa – steady – you're all right now – right hand down and away you go . . .'

Claire waved her hand in thanks as she drove off and in her rear-view mirror she saw the young man cross the road and stride towards Thackeray Buildings. The world wasn't all bad after all, not when there were attractive, smiling men like that around. But poor Mrs Flack probably didn't see many of his sort. She wondered what Gary Flack was like . . . perhaps he was in trouble with the police – could easily be – and his wife wouldn't necessarily want to tell Claire about that. Claire sighed – the Flack story was only just beginning – and as her mind turned back to the depressed, obese young woman in flat thirty-eight, a premonition of doom seemed to envelop her. Then her mind turned back to Francis . . .

Francis slept until late that morning and when he woke he lay still for a while with his eyes shut, listening for sounds of Claire in the kitchen. Funny thing was he couldn't hear her. He wondered what time it was. Unlike him to wake up before Claire's alarm clock went off. He stretched out a foot to feel if Claire was still in bed. There was no one else in the bed. What on earth was the time then? He supposed he'd better open his eyes. He'd think about that in a minute. Claire must be in the bathroom, after all she would hardly have left for work without waking him

[45]

and making him a cup of tea. But there were no sounds from the bathroom. Odd. He turned over and tried to go back to sleep. But he felt surprisingly unsleepy. He really would have to open his eyes – in fact it was becoming almost more of an effort to keep them shut. He opened them and put his hand out to the bedside table for his watch.

Christ! It was half-past eleven. He scratched his head. What the hell was going on? Why hadn't Claire woken him before she left? He felt a shrinking feeling of cold fear and then a swelling surge of panic. Christ! What if she'd had enough of him? He could never manage without her. What would he do? He began to gasp for breath and to reach for his ventilator at the same time. As he fumbled for it, he knocked over the bedside lamp, breaking the bulb, and sent a handful of change and his cigarettes flying to the floor. At last, with relief, his hand closed around the ventilator.

When the attack had finally subsided, Francis got up, dressed and lit a cigarette. It was clear from the state of the flat, which was just as usual, that Claire had not left in any permanent sense, but he was still puzzled by her going like that, without a word. Francis glanced at his watch. It was midday – too late for a cup of tea – he would go down to the pub and have a drink, after what had happened this morning he needed a drink. As he sauntered towards the pub he thought about Claire's behaviour. How dared she just walk out on him like that? She knew he was prone to asthma attacks – she didn't realise how lucky she was not being an asthmatic – it was all right for her. But he couldn't understand what had happened. Why should she do a thing like that? If he'd annoyed her in some way then she should have said so. Anyway, what on earth could he have done to upset her? He was beginning to feel quite angry when a faint recollection of a telephone call in the night came to him. Something to do with Roddy?

Yes, that was it, he was sure that in the middle of the night, while he had been half asleep, he had heard her talking to Roddy. Bloody Roddy. At least that explained it.

[46]

She'd probably had to dash out in a hurry on some silly errand of her brother's.

As he settled down with his first pint in front of him, Francis wondered why the hell Roddy couldn't pull himself together. Get a grip on himself. He caused nothing but anxiety to his family – he was so selfish, and not just selfish but lazy. Lazy – that was it really – Roddy was bone idle . . .

'How's the jewellery-making going then?'

Francis started out of his reverie. The publican was standing in front of him with both hands leaning on the bar.

'Oh that – the jewellery-making did you say? Yes, well, all right thanks – I mean it – er – it hasn't taken off yet sort of thing –' Francis was glad to be interrupted by a man coming up to the bar to order a drink.

Oh God, he must do something about that this afternoon. He really must. He put his face in his hands. If he didn't, Claire could reasonably be quite annoyed when she came back after work. Again he could imagine her hurt, crestfallen face. He really would go down to the Tech in the afternoon.

'Could I have another pint of the same, please?' he said, turning back to the publican.

CHAPTER V

By the time the pub closed Francis had had a few too many again. He felt slightly annoyed with himself about it – he had really only meant to have a couple of pints, but even in his bemused state he realised that one pint was enough to weaken the will – and two, even more so. He must stop drinking so much in the middle of the day. That was basically what prevented him from getting anything done – like signing on at the Tech.

The drink brought with it a vague feeling of euphoria and optimism so that the thought of the Tech didn't plunge him into the usual gloom. In fact the bloody Tech was just a weight around his neck. Why should he go down there? It had never been a really serious idea – just something that had come to them while they were on holiday. He was under no obligation whatsoever to stick to that plan. Of course Claire wouldn't mind. She would hate him to do something he wasn't interested in. Why on earth had he got so worked up about it in the first place?

Francis was strolling back towards the flat, casually looking in shop windows as he passed when he reached W. H. Smith. He decided he might as well go in and have a look around.

He spent about half an hour looking at the periodicals. There was quite an interesting article in one of the women's magazines on understanding your out-of-work man. Claire ought to read that. She probably didn't realise how vulnerable he felt. It was all very well her doing all that social work but sometimes she didn't see what was right under her nose. Of course he had feelings of inadequacy – and of course those feelings of inadequacy undermined his sex drive. Francis suddenly became conscious of a faint tickle and a vague ache at the back of his throat. He swallowed. Bugger that – it felt like the beginnings of a sore throat and a sore throat meant a cold.

A cold was never any good for his sex life. He swallowed again, hoping the symptoms would go away, and went on reading.

When he had finished the article which really was exceptionally perceptive, he glanced at the by-line at the top – he would like to know the woman who had written that – she must be quite someone. Fenella Flint-Pickle. Well, good for Fenella Flint-Pickle. Fenella Flint-Pickle wouldn't have walked out on him first thing in the morning without even making him a cup of tea. He felt like buying the magazine and leaving it around in the flat so that Claire would find it, but it cost over a pound and anyway he couldn't really be bothered.

Francis put the magazine back in its place and wandered over to the music department where he spent some time vaguely looking through tapes of soul music before moving on to the stationery department and staring blankly at the mountains of A4 paper piled neatly beside some vividly coloured student files. He loved paper, especially pads of clean, lined writing paper. He longed to have something to write on the smooth surface.

He felt a twinge of embarrassment as he remembered his past enthusiasm for bridges. But, no, seriously, bridges had not been a very good idea. Something else would suit him better – he wasn't yet sure what; all the same, he picked up a pad of A4 and carried it over to the pay desk. He was about to pay for it when he remembered that he probably didn't have a pen at home. When he had finally chosen the right Pentel – it took him some time to decide whether to have a 'fine' or an 'extra fine' nib – he took the pen and paper back to the pay desk where there was quite a long queue which involved a tedious wait of some four or five minutes, eventually paid and left the shop.

As Francis walked on home he felt elated by his purchases, certain in the knowledge that a suitable subject for his studies would soon come to mind, and confident that Claire would be pleased with him for having done something at last.

When he reached the flat it was only just gone four. Claire wouldn't be back for quite a while. He turned on the television and threw himself down on the sofa. He wasn't really concentrating on the children's programmes which were being shown on BBC1, but was wondering what he was going to write about. He lit a cigarette and drew on it deeply. It reminded him unpleasantly of the ache in the back of his throat. But he had other things on his mind. There were a lot of things he might write about. It was just a question of picking the right one.

Suddenly it came to him – in a flash as it were. Of course. Why the hell hadn't he thought of it before? It was perfectly obvious – staring him in the face – and what an idea! He would write a history of soap operas. There had been no history of soap operas in so far as he knew – and what a subject – what vast, unexplored territory. Incredible!

He could hardly wait for Claire to come home, he was so excited at the prospect of telling her his idea. When she heard about this she would completely understand about his reluctance to sign on for the jewellery-making course. He hoped she would anyway – yes – she would – of course she would – she must.

Naturally it would help if he could get a few interviews with some of the stars – Joan Collins for instance. It might be a bit difficult to arrange but he was sure he could manage it somehow. After all those stars were publicity mad, every one of them, and they'd probably be only too

[50]

pleased to talk to him. They might even pay him so as to be sure to get a mention. The whole idea was absolutely brilliant.

Francis looked at his watch. It was only five o'clock. At least another hour before he could expect Claire. He wondered if there was any of that whisky left in the cupboard. After all the whole thing really did call for a bit of a celebration – and it would do his throat good – he'd have a drop now and then when Claire came back she could join him for the other half. She'd be on her way home pretty soon.

Claire had had an exhausting day and she was feeling unusually irritable. On leaving the Flacks she had gone back to her office where she had had a certain amount of paper work to do and then she had spent a trying afternoon with one of her families who had so many problems that it was hard to know which one to concentrate on first. There was a mentally retarded child, an incontinent grandmother, an out-of-work father, a sick mother, and now one of the boys – a thirteen year old – was thought to be involved with a group of school friends in solvent abuse. Claire sometimes wondered if there was anything she could do to alleviate the lot of these poor people or if it was all a waste of time.

As she drove home she turned her mind back to Francis and his problems. At intervals throughout the day she had been annoyed by the thought of him and surprised by how annoyed she felt – she who was usually so calm and in control of things. Her interrupted night must have upset her. She supposed she was just tired. If he had still not gone to the Tech she really would be quite cross. He must try to help himself a little – she couldn't do everything for him.

But if only Francis would do something for himself – anything – it would be such a relief. How could she be expected to cope with all the weaklings and glue sniffers and single parent families and baby bashers and wife beaters in the area – and then come home to look after Francis as if he were a deprived child? Of course he had been a deprived child and her heart bled for the lonely little boy that he once was. But he had never been half so deprived as all the people she had been seeing today. After all, he was intelligent and educated – he ought to be able to help himself a little. She suddenly felt that she would be really angry if, when she reached home, she found that Francis had still not been to the Tech. What on earth else did he have to do all day?

Claire glanced at her watch. It was late and the traffic was bad. Her irritation mounted and she hooted angrily at a red Metro in front of her which failed to move off as the traffic lights changed to green. The Metro jolted to a start and then stalled in the middle of the lights. Claire began to hate the neat, grey-haired back of the driver's head. Normally she would have been sorry for the poor man, starting and stalling his way through the rush-hour traffic but today she just wished he would get on and pull himself together – like Francis.

At last the Metro set off again, but not before the lights had turned back to red again. Claire sighed and glanced once more at her watch.

As she climbed the stairs to the flat some twenty minutes later she wondered if Francis would be in. He usually was when she came back from work but then she didn't usually leave in the morning without waking him and giving him a cup of tea. He might even be still in bed, she thought crossly as she turned the key in the lock.

'There you are!' exclaimed Francis as she stepped through the door and slammed it shut behind her. 'I wondered where on earth you had got to.'

He came towards her with his arms out.

Claire turned away and pushed him aside with an aggravated gesture and walked into the kitchen.

'I must have a cup of tea,' she said, 'I've had a dreadful day and I'm exhausted.' She flung her bag down on the table.

'What's the matter with you?' asked Francis, as he followed her into the kitchen.

[52]

Claire switched on the kettle and looked around for the teapot. She could hear the maddening sound of the television coming from the sitting room. It sounded like *Crossroads* or some such nonsense. For her own part she had enough of real life dramas not to want to hear about imaginary ones.

'Can't you turn the television off,' she said, pressing the palm of her hand to her brow and shutting her eyes. 'I've got an awful headache.' Well it was almost as if she had with that terrible tinny noise and those idiotic voices echoing around her. She poured the boiling water into the teapot and Francis went to turn off the television.

'Want a cup of tea?' she said grudgingly when he came back.

Francis had a glass of whisky in the other room – his second. Claire had been so late that he had begun to worry. No wonder he'd had a second drink. But he wanted to please her.

'Yes, that'd be nice,' he said. 'I could do with a cup of tea.'

'So what did you do today?' Claire asked aggressively as she sat down at the kitchen table with her tea and pushed a mug towards Francis.

Francis sat down, pulled the teapot towards him and began to pour tea into his pink mug.

'More to the point, what did *you* do?' he asked as he put down the teapot and pushed it idly away from him. 'Milk please.'

Claire handed him the carton.

'I didn't see you this morning,' Francis went on. 'What happened?'

Claire glanced at him. The first gulp of hot tea had begun to calm her nerves and to assuage her aggravation. She put her hand out and touched Francis's.

'Oh Francis,' she said.

Francis added the milk to his tea and two teaspoonfuls of sugar. As he did so Claire gazed at his perfect, delicate profile. Sometimes he made her feel so sad and it was at times like that that she knew he really needed her. She must try not to be so impatient with him. She felt really mean.

'So what happened today?' she asked again in a softer voice.

Relieved by the gentleness of her tone, Francis turned and looked at her. He loved her round, broad face and thick, straight, dark brown hair and he loved the rosy intensity of her caring expression. It was all right after all.

'I've had this wonderful idea,' he said. 'It's absolutely brilliant. I can't think why I never thought of it before. It just came to me – like that – out of the blue, as I was sitting on the sofa in there.' He pointed towards the sitting room.

'Well, come on then, what is it?' Claire asked.

'The thing is you may not realise at first quite what a good idea it is. But, I promise you, it can't fail. You see it's a subject which is bound to interest hundreds of people – thousands – all over the world. It'll probably get translated into dozens of foreign languages. Think of all those translation rights!'

Claire felt a wave of despair flood over her.

'Never mind the translation rights, just tell me what it is,' she said. Images of cantilever bridges kept somehow forcing themselves into her brain.

Francis lit a cigarette and inhaled deeply.

'You see,' he said, 'no one has ever written a good history of soap operas.'

'Soap operas! You want to write a history of soap operas?'

'And why ever not?' Francis was cross. The trouble with Claire was that she never had any faith in him. Who was she to say that he couldn't do it? She didn't know anything about writing books, after all she had only written reports on problem families. A book was quite a different matter. He had the time, the enthusiasm and certainly the know-how. He had read quite a lot one way and another and certainly had an idea or two about how such a book should be put together. What did she mean by being so negative? What she needed, now he came to think of it, was to read an

[54]

article he'd read somewhere recently about understanding unemployed men. It was all very well Claire understanding all these wife beaters and child molesters – but what about him? Didn't he deserve a bit of her understanding and sympathy – or did she just keep that for work?

Francis had gone quite pink in the face.

'I never said you couldn't do it,' said Claire. 'I was just thinking that . . . well . . .' She didn't want to say anything about bridges. 'Well – are you sure that writing a book is what you really want to do? I mean, it would be awfully lonely. That's what would be so good about doing something at the Tech. As well as learning something, you'd be getting out and meeting people . . .'

Francis interrupted.

'I've had enough of hearing about the Tech,' he almost shouted. 'I've had the Tech up to here,' he said, tapping his forehead with the side of his hand as if in a naval salute. 'Up to here.' He tapped his head again. 'You just think that because you're a social worker, you can come home and patronise me and talk about the Tech. Well I don't need your so-called understanding and sympathy. You can keep that for your work . . .'

'I never patronised you,' said Claire. 'I'm just trying to help – to look at the problem from all sides. Let's have another cup of tea.' She picked up the pot. 'It needs more water.' She stood up and took it over to the kettle. 'Shall we just sit down and talk things over sensibly?'

'That's exactly what I've been trying to do, but you won't listen to me. You just despise me. Anybody can see that. And where did you go this morning without saying good-bye, I'd like to know? And don't you realise that it's extremely bad for a man's ego to be despised and it's particularly bad for a man who is out of work. You can emasculate a person,' he added, warming to Fenella Flint-Pickle's theme. 'I suppose you don't know that a man's libido is directly affected by his performance in the office . . .'

What on earth was Francis getting so cross about? Claire

[55]

had rarely known him to be so worked up. Sometimes he was depressed or moody, he even cried when things seemed to be getting too much for him, but all this anger was quite unusual.

Claire filled up the teapot, brought it back to the table and sat down.

'Now you may quite rightly point out,' Francis went on, 'that if a man hasn't got an office, he can hardly have a performance in it.' All this talking wasn't doing his sore throat any good. 'But that doesn't alter the fact that a man's performance in his office can be vitally important to him in more ways than one.'

Claire wished that Francis would stop saying 'performance' and 'office'. It was terribly annoying and sounded rather silly.

'And if I did have an office my performance in it would probably boost my ego and give me all the confidence which I need, but as I don't have an office, my performance in it can't be measured, and if I were to write this book, my performance writing the book would be the equivalent to my performance in an office if I had one . . .'

'For God's sake, stop talking such nonsense!' exclaimed Claire.

'There you are,' Francis's voice rose, 'you say you want to talk sensibly about things and you're not even prepared to listen for one minute. All you want to do is to patronise me and to boss me because you despise me.'

His throat was really beginning to hurt and he could feel the faint pricking of tears behind his eyes. No one had ever understood him properly. Not even Claire when it came to the crunch. Everyone always thought he was weak – or lazy – or stupid – and of course he wasn't any of those things. It was hardly his fault he was a chronic asthmatic, and he had never asked his mother to abandon him when he was only six. No one realised what a hell of a time he had had with his father. His father was a very insensitive, bullying man who had no insight whatsoever into other people's feelings. No wonder Francis's mother had left him.

[56]

'And if you think I'm talking nonsense,' Francis went on, 'just you go and read this article I was reading this afternoon in some magazine or other – I can't remember what it was called – but one of those magazines. It tells you all about how to understand a person when he's out of work. And I think you should read it and then you'd find out that you don't know everything. This woman who wrote it, she's a really clever woman. She's probably got more understanding of personal problems than all the employees of the social services put together. Just look at them – all these people you work with – a bunch of incompetents – they're always leaving babies to be murdered or to be starved to death . . .' Francis's renewed aggression had helped him to overcome the tears which had been pricking behind his eyes. 'They can't be very proud of their performances in their offices,' he said.

Claire had never known Francis be so violent. She wished he would shut up, he really was giving her a headache. She put out her hand and touched his arm.

'What's the matter, Francis, why are you so upset?'

'Upset! I'm not the one who's upset. What makes you think I'm so upset?' He stood up. 'I'm getting a cold,' he said. 'I've got a bloody awful sore throat and I need a drink.' There was just a drop of whisky left in the bottom of the bottle.

'Well get yourself a drink and come back, and let's talk about the book,' said Claire.

When he had left the room she put her elbows on the table, buried her head in her hands and sighed deeply. How could she ever get through to him? No one would be happier than she if he had a job or wrote a book or whatever but he needed to get out of the flat and do something with other people. He hadn't been able even to get started on the book about bridges despite all the encouragement she'd given him. And soap operas didn't seem much better than bridges.

Francis came back into the kitchen with his drink in one hand and a cigarette in the other.

[57]

'You don't really believe in me,' he said as he sat down. 'You say you do, but you don't – and how can I expect you to when I haven't yet done anything to give you any reason to?' He stared at her with his great, sad, blue eyes.

'Of course I believe in you,' said Claire, covering his hand with hers. 'You know I do.' She looked sorrowfully back at him.

'You see, I just know that this thing about soap operas is a brilliant idea. It's got to be. There's never been a book about soap operas before . . .'

'How do you know?'

'What do you mean, how do I know? There just hasn't. I'm sure there hasn't. Have you ever seen a book about soap operas?'

'No, I haven't, but . . .'

'There you are then. And I'm going to write one and it's going to be a best-seller . . .'

'You'll have to make sure there hasn't been one, you know, and then, well, I don't want to be unkind, but you must remember how when you wanted to write that other book, you found it so difficult to get down to work. Couldn't you do something else as well – like the jewellery thing – and then write the book in your spare time?' Claire was exhausted, she wished they didn't have to have this conversation that evening and besides she was hungry. She stood up again and went to look in the refrigerator to see what there was to eat.

'Supper,' said Francis. 'There you are, all you can think of is supper just when I'm telling you about one of the most important decisions of my life. And why? Because you don't believe in me. If you believed in me you wouldn't go harping back to bridges. Bridges were different. They were obviously different. Can't you see the difference between bridges and soap operas?'

'You know I believe in you. Do I really have to keep saying so over and over again?' Despite the emphasis in Claire's voice, the tone seemed to fail to carry the necessary conviction.

'Yes you do have to keep saying so,' Francis nearly yelled as he pushed his glass of whisky angrily off the side of the table onto the floor. He stood up and kicked the pieces of broken glass. 'Of course you have to keep saying so. And now there's no more bloody whisky,' he said and burst into tears.

Claire couldn't take any more. If she stayed she would lose her temper, so she quite simply shut the refrigerator door, picked up her bag and coat and made for the front door.

'I've got to get out,' she said. 'I'll call you in the morning.'

As she ran down the stairs, struggling to put her coat on, large tears welled up in Claire's eyes and rolled down her cheeks. She had never walked out on Francis before and she hated herself for doing it because she knew that she was the stronger of the two. But she could not stay there feeling as she did and listen to him endlessly trying to pick a quarrel. Poor Francis. Poor, poor Francis. It was only natural that he should feel nervous and tense – without a job – without anything to do when he got up in the morning. As she climbed into her little green car and inserted the key in the ignition she hoped he would be all right. There were some sausages in the fridge and some tomatoes. Should she go back? It was so cruel to leave him alone. But if she went back that dreadful argument would only start up again. No. She would go round to her mother's. It would probably be better that way. But as she drove she felt appallingly guilty and huge tears streamed and streamed down her cheeks.

When Nancy opened the front door she was amazed to see her daughter. The last person she had been thinking about was Claire. She and George had been watching the television news. Well, George had been asleep, of course, but Nancy had been knitting and daydreaming about David Owen. David Owen was terribly handsome. Just the sort of man she would have liked to have an affair with. She blushed at the indecency of her own mind.

[59]

What would Claire think of her mother if she could read her thoughts?

'What a lovely surprise,' she said, 'how lovely to see you,' and she kissed her daughter.

CHAPTER VI

When Nancy's affair with Gregory Finch ended so
abruptly, there was no doubt about it that her heart was
broken. She had never for a moment supposed, as she lay
romancing on her bed, listening to the record of *South
Pacific*, playing 'Some Enchanted Evening' over and over
again and dreaming of an illusory airman with a forage cap
perched on the side of his head, that the end of a love affair
could be so painful. The loneliness, the humiliation and the
sense of loss seemed quite unbearable. She supposed that
that was almost how her mother must have felt when her
father was killed in the Battle of Britain, and she began to
sympathise vaguely with her, or at least to feel rather guilty
at what had been her own lack of understanding at the
time. But most of all she thought about herself. She
wondered what had gone wrong and she asked herself over
and over again whether Gregory had ever had any real
intention of marrying her.

She was sure that he had and was easily convinced by his
explanation that he could not leave his neurotic mother to
live on her own. A sense of duty or rather a misplaced sense
of guilt had bound him until her death to an agoraphobic
woman in her middle age who might well live another
thirty years. Sometimes Nancy played with the idea of
getting in touch with Gregory again and telling him that

there was no place for such guilt. It was not his fault about his mother and he could hardly be expected to sacrifice his whole life to her. Nancy didn't really wonder at the time what Gregory's mother would in fact do without her son. In fact she had very little understanding of the condition of agoraphobia, vaguely presuming that with an effort of the will it could be overcome. Or if Mrs Finch were really so sick, perhaps she would be better off in hospital.

Then in moments of agonising doubt Nancy would ask herself if Gregory hadn't just been making excuses. Perhaps he never really loved her at all and once he had made love to her he had begun to despise her. Then she felt dreadfully guilty about that too and afraid that she would bear the burden of her wickedness for the rest of her life. Not that her life seemed to have any meaning any more. The whole country was in a fever of optimistic excitement about the dawning of a new Elizabethan era and the papers were filled with talk of the forthcoming Coronation of the young Queen, but Nancy could conceive of no reason for rejoicing.

She went wearily and automatically to work at her new job as secretary in a firm selling fire extinguishers, and spent her evenings and weekends moping in her bedroom, no longer even playing her records but lying on her bed, staring at the ceiling and smoking Craven A cigarettes. She had only taken up smoking – to the intense irritation of Mrs Larders who didn't like to see women smoking – since her heart was broken.

Nancy's mother, busy with her job and her own nostalgic sorrow, didn't really notice the change that had come over her daughter although from time to time it did strike her that perhaps the girl ought to be getting out a bit more. One day she would need to find a husband, but then she was only young and there was plenty of time for that yet. She hadn't married until her late twenties herself, and she had been blissfully happy.

After a few months Mrs Larders, who did not like to think of the child picking up with any young man she met in her office and who had been initially delighted by the apparent turn of events, began to be irritated by Nancy's gloomy air and by the permanent silence which emanated from her bedroom. She thought, and told Nancy's mother so, that the time had come to look for a husband for the girl. She felt that it was somehow incumbent on her to introduce her grand-daughter to suitable young men, but she wasn't at all sure where to find them.

So for months Nancy went nowhere but to work until even her old school friends gave up begging her to come to the cinema with them. Then one evening towards the end of May her oldest and best friend came round to call.

Mrs Larders was somewhat surprised as she did not like casual callers and had always made that quite plain to Nancy, but Heather was a well brought up girl with good manners so Mrs Larders, having glowered at her unin-vitingly as she opened the door, asked her to come in.

'Wait in the sitting room, dear,' she said. 'I'll fetch Nancy. It will do the child good to see you.'

Nancy came down from her bedroom, amazed that Heather had so bravely confronted her grandmother. Her friends had always been terrified of Mrs Larders.

Heather wanted Nancy to go for a walk with her. It was a lovely evening and the two girls hadn't seen each other for ages. She said that she had come in on the spur of the moment – she had just been passing by that way.

Nancy was really rather glad. Her bedroom was becoming quite boring and after all it was a beautiful evening, the trees were in blossom and spring was at last well and truly in the air.

As the two girls walked and talked Nancy suddenly began to feel quite happy – or at least not unhappy – and interested in the local gossip. Two of her old school friends were engaged and would be getting married in the autumn. Heather herself was in love with a wonderful boy but he was doing his national service and was away in Korea. She was terrified for him and his letters did seem to take such ages to reach her. But they were wonderful when they came. Heather hoped that when Martin came home he would find a good job and they would be able to marry. She described the kind of wedding dress she would like: there would be four bridesmaids and Heather's older sister would make the cake.

Heather's gabbling optimism made Nancy laugh. Wasn't she being a bit premature talking about bridesmaids?

The two girls met again for a walk a few days later and it was then that Heather suggested that Nancy should come with her to London to see the Coronation procession.

At first Nancy didn't want to go. It was as though she wished to nurture her broken heart and was unwilling to allow anything to come between her and her sorrow. To a certain extent her broken heart was what made her interesting to herself and she resented the idea of being forced into the mould of an ordinary, happy-go-lucky person. But as Coronation fever mounted Nancy found her will weakening.

Heather and her brother were planning to go to London on the eve of the Coronation, armed with sleeping bags and thermoses of tea, mackintoshes, camping stools, sandwiches and Union Jacks. They would camp on the streets overnight to be sure of a good view in the morning. The route of the procession had already been published in the press and the only thing which remained to be decided was where to pitch camp. Some said that the only place to be was outside the Abbey – others preferred the Mall but Heather was rather in favour of Piccadilly on the grounds that it would be less crowded than the other two more obvious places.

Nancy began to feel quite excited by the whole idea and eventually agreed to go, partly because she felt that if she didn't she might regret it for a long time to come.Surprisingly enough Mrs Larders rather encouraged the idea. Heather was a nice child and her brother, who was several years older would see that no harm came to the girls, not that much harm was likely to come to them in a crowd. Much as Mrs Larders had disapproved of Nancy's sly ways the year before, she thought that the girl had punished herself enough. All this moping around was thoroughly selfish and did no one any good. Mrs Larders had of course made enquiries about Heather's brother. He sounded like a sensible young man – not the irresponsible sort at all, but a nice boy who still lived with his family who were decent people, pillars of the local church; and he had held down a sensible job in Barclays Bank for several years now. Mrs Larders never went to church herself, as she couldn't find the time, but she generally approved of those that did. You never knew but something might even come of the meeting, and Mrs Larders was anxious to see the girl settled.

Once Nancy had decided to go she became tremendously excited. Nothing had delighted her so much for a long time. She and Heather met frequently to finalise their plans.

Although Nancy had known Heather for most of her school years she had only just seen her brother on a few occasions. He was several years older than the two girls and had been away first at school and then doing his military service. He was a dull-looking boy, Nancy thought, tall and lanky, with a pale face and heavy horn-rimmed spectacles. She knew that he worked in one of the banks, Barclays perhaps – she wasn't sure – and had once or twice seen him driving by in his battered old Ford Prefect. Anyway she wasn't going to be interested in him because she was still in love with Gregory – or so she fondly imagined – and would be for the rest of her life.

The weather forecast on June 1st was extremely depressing. It seemed unlikely that the grey clouds would lift in time to allow even one ray of light to shine on the young Queen and her people, but no amount of heavy cloud or pouring rain could discourage Heather and Nancy from setting out although Heather's brother was worried that the girls might catch cold and might find the long wet vigil too much for them. He, of course, had done part of his military service in Malaya after which experience a rainy night on a London pavement would be a piece of cake.

The train into London was packed with enthusiastic people all looking for the best positions along the route and all, like Nancy, Heather and her brother, armed with jerseys and mackintoshes, umbrellas and gumboots.

They did not sleep much that night in their chosen position by Green Park tube station. There was singing and laughing and cheering and even drinking as Heather's brother produced half a bottle of whisky from his mackintosh pocket. The whisky warmed them even more than the hot tea from their thermos and certainly added to their high spirits. At around four o'clock in the morning the three finally fell into restless, uncomfortable sleep, huddled close together in their sleeping bags and leaning against the railings of Green Park.

Only a few hours later they were awake again. It was raining but still more and more people were pouring into the streets. There was a feeling of tense suppressed excitement and then suddenly, a murmur rose from the crowd and spread and swelled until it became a babble. The suppressed excitement was about to be unleashed. Nancy struggled to her feet and strained her neck to see what it was all about just as a resounding, full-throated cheer of sheer joy burst, it seemed, from the whole of London. Someone was waving an early morning paper. Nancy caught sight of the headline: 'Crowning Glory, Everest Climbed!'

'Hurrah! Hurrah!' she yelled with the rest. Nothing at that moment was further from her mind than her old broken heart.

It barely stopped raining all day. But no one allowed the weather to dampen their spirits as they all remained cheerful and happy throughout the long waiting hours. The slightest little incidents caused immense mirth – a pigeon settling on an old man's head, faces appearing at the windows of the buildings opposite the park, a postman on a bicycle long after the street was closed to traffic, a newsvendor shouting about Sherpa Tensing and Edmund Hillary, a fat lady from the Midlands wearing a bathing-cap to protect

[66]

her perm from the weather. There was always something to look at. Two Australians who had also camped by the tube station that night made friends with Nancy and Heather. They all shared sandwiches and tea and sang 'Waltzing Matilda'. The Australians had never been to Britain before but were not in the least put out by the weather as they had frequently been told that it always rained in England and so had come fully prepared.

A renewed thrill of excitement stirred the crowd when the Royal Engineers came to take up their positions lining the route. Someone had brought a wireless and people danced to Victor Sylvester's band and then fell quiet to listen to a description of the scene in the Abbey as the peers and peeresses took up their positions, dressed in ermine and velvet. And later the Coronation service itself was relayed.

The time didn't seem to drag at all but as the bands of the Durham Light Infantry and the Royal Scots Fusiliers finally appeared at around three o'clock, trotting up the street from Piccadilly Circus, at the head of the great procession, there was a renewed surge of joyous cheering. The long procession seemed to go past in a flash and when it was all over Nancy was left only with a vivid impression of the highlights. Winston Churchill making the old victory sign, the fat Queen of Tonga smiling in the rain, and the tumultuous crescendo of cheering which greeted the golden coach drawn by eight grey horses and carrying the newly anointed Queen crowned in the Imperial State crown with the Orb and Sceptre at her side.

Nancy and Heather and even Heather's brother were all completely swept up in the magic of the moment. They cheered and chanted and waved their flags with the best and when the procession had finally passed they gathered up their things and made their way, carried along by the tide of the crowd, to the Mall and up to the Victoria Monument, where they stood tightly crushed against each other in the throng singing and shouting, 'We want the Queen!' until she appeared on the balcony and another mighty cheer broke from the people.

[67]

George, Heather's brother, was worried that they might all lose each other in the crowd. They were carrying quite a lot and so it was not easy to hold on to each other, but as they walked slowly up the Mall Nancy suddenly realised that she seemed to be holding George's hand which was a peculiar thing to be doing. She glanced up at the side of his plain boney face, just as he turned to look at her. He smiled almost conspiratorially and it occurred to her that behind his horn-rimmed spectacles he had quite nice brown eyes. She rather liked holding his hand and gladly returned the pressure when he squeezed hers. She didn't even give a thought to Gregory as she was swept along in the crowd under the rain, but, light-headed with exhaustion, gazed up contentedly, rather than happily, at lanky George.

When they all finally reached home late that evening, George kissed Nancy on the cheek as he left her at her door, squeezed her hand again and murmured in her ear, 'See you soon.'

Heather, dazed with exhaustion, hardly took in what was going on at all.

For the rest of the week no one at work or at home talked of anything but the Coronation. Everyone seemed either to have seen it on the television or to have heard it on the wireless and some, like Nancy, had been to London and camped in the rain drenched streets.

Mrs Larders was really rather proud of her grand-daughter. She thought that Nancy had shown initiative, and in any case she strongly approved of patriotism.

When the weekend came George telephoned and invited Nancy to the cinema with him. They were showing *Roman Holiday* at the Odeon with Gregory Peck and a wonderful new actress called Audrey Hepburn. Nancy had heard of *Roman Holiday* and longed to see it. It was all about a Princess running away from her entourage and falling in love with a journalist. It was supposed to be based on Princess Margaret.

She told her grandmother that she was going to the cinema with George and wondered what the reaction would be.

[68]

Mrs Larders was quite pleased. She had had a look at George and he seemed like a presentable young man. A possible marriage partner even, and it was time to get the girl off her hands.

Nancy began to go out regularly with George and although she did not feel swept away by passion as she had done with Gregory, she soon grew fond of him and looked forward eagerly to seeing him at the weekends. George was kind and thoughtful and extremely gentlemanly. In fact he was rather a serious young man with a strong religious faith who went regularly to church and sometimes he took Nancy with him to Evensong.

Although she had been educated at a Catholic convent, Nancy had never been very interested in religion. Neither her grandmother nor her mother ever went to church and she herself had usually regarded church as rather boring. She supposed that God might exist in a benign sort of way but she never really felt that he had any relevance to her, yet when she went to Evensong with George she began to feel the guilt about her 'past' more strongly than ever. She thought that she would quite like to marry George and she supposed that that was perhaps what he had in mind but what would he think of her if he knew? She earnestly wished that the past could be undone and she loathed the burden of her guilt. Perhaps if George found out he would refuse to have anything more to do with her.

At the general confession she would close her eyes tightly and bury her face in her hands, muttering the words with a new-found fervour and addressing them to a new-found, if vague, presence:

'We have erred and strayed from Thy ways like lost sheep . . . We have offended against Thy holy laws . . . We have done those things which we ought not to have done; and there is no health in us . . .'

Somehow the prayer seemed to soothe her troubled conscience.

Mrs Larders thought it thoroughly suitable that George should take Nancy to church. He was obviously a serious young man, not at all like some of these thoughtless young people there were around these days.

'And talking of thoughtless young people,' she said one day at tea, 'Mrs Saunders's grand-daughter has had her baby. She was only married in January which by my calculation makes it a six-months baby.' She snorted. 'Of course the family are all saying that it was born early, but who ever heard of a six-months baby weighing nearly nine pounds?'

Nancy looked down awkwardly at her seed cake.

'Well, you never know these days,' sighed Nancy's mother.

'Never know indeed!' went on Mrs Larders. 'Nobody ever kept an eye on that child. She was no good from the start if you ask me. Up to all sorts of tricks from an early age. Mind you she's lucky to have found a husband at all. Men don't like used goods.' She glowered at Nancy across the table.

Nancy blushed and took a large bite of seed cake. Surely Mrs Larders couldn't know. How could she? No, she was just threatening Nancy, but Nancy remembered those moments in the park which she knew she had enjoyed at the time, and just wished that they hadn't been, for what was that enjoyment compared to the anguish she had endured since?

Mrs Larders was warming to her theme.

'Now that girl should know how lucky she is that the young man married her. I remember thinking at the time that the wedding was arranged in rather a hurry. But as I say, she'd been playing with fire for a long time, and the trouble with these girls who misbehave is that once they fall, they get a taste for it and then there's no holding them and before you can say "Jack Robinson" they've ruined their whole lives and no one will marry them.'

Nancy suddenly felt quite sick. How dare her grandmother sit there talking about getting a 'taste for it'. Nancy herself had acquired the taste and she sometimes wondered if it was not just that which encouraged her to think of marriage to George. She tried to imagine what it would be like with George – he was such a polite sort of person.

'I never cared for Mrs Saunders's grand-daughter,' Mrs Larders droned on, 'a pert girl if you ask me, and as for the young man, he won't have much peace with a wife like that; he'll need eyes in the back of his head I should say.'

'I don't really think that's any business of ours,' Nancy retorted sharply.

'There is no need to be impolite, dear,' Mrs Larders pursed her lips and poured herself another cup of tea.

Nancy's mother said that she had had a long day at work and had a headache. She thought she might go and lie down for half an hour.

That night as she lay in bed Nancy thought long and hard about her guilt. She decided that she had hurt no one but herself by her behaviour and she need never tell anyone about it. She might never know whether the guilt itself sprang from a real feeling that she had done something wrong or whether it was entirely the result of her grandmother's indoctrination. Mrs Larders was quite capable of making Nancy feel guilty about the silliest little things, like leaving the light on in the bathroom or forgetting to change her shoes when she came in from the street.

In many ways Nancy's mother was no better as she had instilled in her daughter as a young child such a terror of displeasing or letting down her father, the dashing airman in the sky who had died for his country, that Nancy's whole childhood and adolescence seemed one way or another to have been riddled with guilt. If Nancy ever had children she would bring them up differently. Then she remembered the girls in the Catholic convent she'd been to – haunted by guilt every one of them – rushing backwards and forwards to confession all the time.

No, Nancy's children would be brought up guilt-free. And as for herself, she must and would put aside her guilt about Gregory forever, and look to the future or otherwise she might go mad.

[71]

Perhaps, she thought as she dozed off into a light sleep, her earnest prayers at Evensong had been answered. 'Restore thou them that are penitent . . .'; but how could she be penitent if she didn't think that she had done anything wrong?

CHAPTER VII

Nancy really was surprised to see Claire. She had been so lost in her daydream about David Owen that it took her a moment or two to readjust herself. Claire looked distraught and it was fairly obvious that there had been some sort of a crisis which was surprising in itself as Nancy regarded her daughter as being infinitely calm and, besides, it never occurred to her that Claire and Francis ever really quarrelled. But clearly something was the matter.

George, and the dog at his feet, both stirred in their sleep at the sound of voices; George half opened his eyes and then, on seeing Claire, woke up completely with something of a start. The dog jumped up and wagged its tail in greeting, shifting its weight excitedly from paw to paw as it did so, and dribbling from its jaws.

'We were just watching the news,' George said, struggling to his feet and glancing at the television where David Owen was still holding forth. 'I rather think your mother has a bit of a weakness for the smarmy doctor.' He leaned over and turned off the television.

Nancy turned away and blushed. She was surprised that George had noticed her liking for David Owen. There was no harm in it, of course, and as she had told herself time and time again there was no harm either in fantasising about him. Why could she never rid herself of her ridiculous feelings of guilt?

She went into the kitchen to make a cup of coffee for her daughter. At least Claire and Roddy weren't riddled with guilt. At least she had done that for them. She could hardly imagine Claire fretting about a few idle thoughts which passed through her head. After all, she thought defiantly as she poured the boiling water onto the coffee, George had really been rather a disappointing lover over the years, so why shouldn't she allow herself a little idle fantasy? And then she felt a pang of guilt for having entertained so disloyal a thought. For George had always been a kind and considerate husband.

As she carried the coffee into the sitting room she brought her thoughts back to reality – after all Claire seemed to be in trouble – and she obviously needed her parents' help.

Claire didn't really want to discuss her problems about Francis with her parents as she thought it would be rather mean but she had to produce some explanation for her sudden arrival and for her wish to stay the night.

'Sorry to burst in on you like this,' she said when her mother returned with the coffee. 'But as I was just telling Dad, I've had rather a tiring day and Francis was busy when I got back so I thought you wouldn't mind if I came round.'

'Busy!' said Nancy. 'What's he up to then?' George, she could see, was busy lighting his pipe but she didn't imagine that Francis was ever even as busy as that. She looked at her daughter who had obviously been crying and said,

'Sit down and have a nice cup of coffee and tell us about it.'

Claire sat down and sighed.

'Have you had anything to eat, darling?' her mother asked. 'We haven't eaten yet and there's a stew in the oven.'

Claire said she'd love to share it with them.

There was an awkward silence for a while as they all sipped their coffee.

[74]

Then George said, 'You look a bit upset, old girl – anything the matter?'

'No – no – not really. I'm just exhausted and – well – Francis has started writing.'

'Oh how wonderful!' Nancy felt really pleased. George merely raised one laconic eyebrow. 'But I thought he'd given up thinking about those bridges a long time ago,' said Nancy.

'Oh, no, he's not writing about bridges,' said Claire. 'He's got an entirely new project.'

'What's that then?' her mother asked.

Suddenly and for no apparent reason Claire burst into tears. 'I'm so sorry,' she sobbed, 'to be such a bore – it's just that – well it's all really so silly – so silly – ' and she went on crying.

George was rather embarrassed. He hated to see women crying, partly because he always felt sorry for them and never knew how to deal with the situation and partly because they looked so ugly doing it. Nancy got up and went and sat beside her daughter on the sofa and put her arms around her.

'What you need,' she said, 'is a stiff drink. George, get Claire a drop of whisky will you, dear?'

George was delighted to be of some use and shuffled away with the dog at his heels to fetch the whisky decanter from the dining room. It upset him to see Claire so unhappy, but what could you expect with that lazy, good-for-nothing Francis? He was a likeable enough boy but he needed to be a bit more than likeable if he was to make anything of his life – or if he was to make Claire happy. Sometimes George thought Francis was a waste of rations.

Nancy, as she tried to console her daughter, was thinking that perhaps it was just as well after all that Claire and Francis weren't married. Perhaps this was the beginning of a break-up and then after a while – Claire would obviously be unhappy for a bit – someone more suitable than Francis would turn up. Someone a couple of years older than Claire – someone with a job and a car – someone who would look

[75]

after her – someone altogether more substantial than Francis in every way – financially, mentally and physically.

Just as George came back with a glass of whisky for Claire there was a sharp ring at the front door.

'Good Lord!' said Nancy, 'who on earth can that be now?'

George went into the hall with the dog bounding ahead of him, wagging its tail and barking.

There were two policemen on the front doorstep.

'Good evening, sir,' they both said as George opened the door.

'We were wondering, sir, if you could inform us as to the whereabouts of a certain Mr Roderick Potter,' one of the policemen asked.

'Roddy! What do you want Roddy for?' George felt the faintest twinge of fear. The thought of Roddy always made George feel apprehensive – not that he ever said so to anyone else – not even to Nancy. He just kept his counsel and hoped for the best.

'Perhaps we might just step inside for a moment and have a word with you,' the policeman went on.

'Yes, do please come in,' said George, opening the door wider.

The two policemen stepped over the threshold side by side, took off their hats with their right hands and put them under their left arms, smoothed their hair with their right hands and stood awkwardly side by side. One of them was large and fat, the other smaller and much thinner. Laurel and Hardy thought George, and almost simultaneously the answer to two down in the crossword came to him in a flash – it was obviously 'laurustinus' – how stupid of him not to have realised before.

'Nights are drawing in, sir,' said Hardy.

Laurel bent to pat George's slobbering dog on the head, and said, 'Nice dog you have there.' And to the dog, 'Good boy.'

'Come on in then,' said George ushering the two men into the sitting room where a startled Nancy and a flustered Claire were hastily trying to regain their composure.

'Good evening ladies,' said the two policemen, and the fat one continued:

'We was hoping as how you might be able to help us as to the whereabouts of a certain Mr Roderick Potter, sir. We believe the gentleman to be your son, and would like to question him on account of how he might be able to give evidence for us concerning a small matter.'

Nancy was appalled. She had hardly recovered from the surprise of seeing Claire arrive in floods of tears and now there were these two mumbling fools standing on the carpet and talking about Roddy. She couldn't really take in what it was they wanted. Roddy could hardly be in trouble with the police. Well, she knew that he was liable to get himself into all sorts of silly scrapes but surely never anything serious – certainly nothing criminal. Roddy was immature – a slow developer – there was no doubt about that and it was high time he began to show some signs of growing up. After all he was over thirty now and had never had what anyone might call a serious job or, so far as anyone knew, a serious girlfriend, either. A lot of rather pretty, tarty little things and, Nancy suspected, a married woman or two.

'He can't have done anything wrong, can he?' Nancy asked.

'Oh no, madam. Do not concern yourself on that account,' answered the policeman. 'It is merely that Mr Roderick Potter's motorcar, a red Porsche bearing the registration number AYD 37X, was observed parked in Orchard Close between approximately twenty-three hundred hours last evening and two-thirty am this morning. There has been a burglary in the Close and it is not unlikely that Mr Roderick Potter being something of a night bird, if you get my meaning, madam' – the policeman cleared his throat and paused awkwardly – 'might be in a position to advise us as to what he saw. It is not impossible that unbeknown to himself, Mr Roderick Potter may have observed, not to say witnessed, the criminals making their getaway. It is to this effect that we would like to question your son, madam. Unfortunately the lady with whom Mr Roderick Potter was visiting' – the policeman cleared his throat again and turned his head slightly so as to address his words on this rather indelicate subject to George – 'is at the present time unable to advise us as to the whereabouts of the gentleman.'

George wondered why it was that policemen couldn't talk like normal people. Or perhaps this was just a particularly stupid policeman. Not that his mate looked much brighter.

'I'm very sorry,' said George, 'but we haven't seen my son for a couple of weeks. Of course as soon as he gets in touch we will tell him to drop round and see you.'

'We have attempted to contact him at his permanent address but it would appear that Mr Roderick Potter is temporarily absent from those premises – in fact, we have been informed that the gentleman is not infrequently absent from that address. Hence it would not be unreasonable to conjecture that it is not always as simple as might be expected to trace the gentleman.'

'I've certainly had that problem myself,' said George who was beginning to feel rather irritated by the two policemen.

'Could you be so kind, sir, just to enlighten us as to Mr Roderick Potter's place of work? We might perhaps be able to pop in and bother him in his office.' The policeman smirked.

'I'm afraid that my son is out of work at the moment, as far as I know,' said George, his irritation mounting. 'Now Officer, if that is all that I can do for you . . .' George moved towards the door.

The police officer, taking the hint, thanked George for his kind co-operation and wished Nancy and Claire a very good night before leaving the room with his companion.

Nancy seemed quite relieved by the policeman's explanation of why they wanted Roddy. Claire, who had said nothing throughout their visit and who was rather glad that they had not seen fit to bring her into the conversation, didn't feel quite so happy as she remembered Roddy's

[78]

angry telephone call in the middle of the night. Of course Roddy was a perfect fool. What was the point in her lying for him if his lady friend was going to tell the police that he was at her house?

Claire wondered what the hell Roddy had in fact been up to. She simply couldn't imagine but she felt unpleasantly sure that they hadn't heard the last of the incident. Oh, her poor parents! How dare she come and burden them with her trifling problems as well?

'Well, well, well,' said George coming back from seeing the policemen off. What a to-do about nothing. I think we deserve a drink all round. Nance, what about you?'

'Yes, dear. I think I could do with a tot. But what about our stew? I think we should all go and eat it before it's burnt to a frazzle.'

As George poured out the drinks his mind returned to the crossword which he had only just begun that day – 'laurustinus' would help a great deal. He would write it in in a moment. Thank the Good Lord there was nothing to worry about where Roddy was concerned. Not this time anyway. The boy might be a bit careless with tax returns and George for one would think twice before buying a second-hand car off him, but it was ridiculous to suppose that he'd been on a burglary. And even Roddy – if he were a burglar – could hardly be so stupid as to leave his particularly noticeable motorcar at the site of the crime for half the night. No, George could go happily back to his own thoughts and if 'laurustinus' was the answer to two down, then the third letter of ten across must be 'u'.

The three of them ate their supper without saying much. Nancy felt that the moment had passed when she could ask Claire what was troubling her although she might have another opportunity later if she found herself alone with Claire – over the washing-up, for instance.

George was glad that the incident had passed without too much having been said. On the whole those damn police-men had called at just the right time. In George's experi-ence, the more people said about things, the worse everything became. You didn't want to go around the place telling everybody your problems. Other people weren't very likely to be able to solve them any better than yourself. Claire and Francis had best settle their own affairs although Claire was of course welcome – more than welcome – at home whenever she cared to turn up. He would ask no questions and it would be just as well if Nancy didn't either.

While Nancy and Claire washed up, George returned to the sitting room where he managed to complete nearly half the crossword before dropping off to sleep.

As she dried the dishes, Claire was talking rather nervously about this and that, keeping Nancy at arm's length, or so it seemed. It was better to say nothing now – perhaps all those tears were just a storm in a teacup.

'Ah well,' said Nancy as she removed her apron, 'I think it's time we all went to bed. I'll wake up your father and he can put the dog out.'

When she was at last in bed, with the light out and ready for sleep, the comforting vision of Dr David Owen loomed up almost uninvited before Nancy's eyes. I don't suppose he snores, she thought, and prodded George gently in the ribs.

Back in her old childhood bedroom, Claire found it hard to sleep. There was too much on her mind. She knew she couldn't do without Francis but more than that she knew that he couldn't do without her, and it was partly this knowledge that he needed her which bound her to him so closely. It was not unnatural, she thought, to love someone because they needed you. But she wished he would find a proper occupation. What on earth did he know about soap operas and the world of television? Perhaps he knew more about them than about bridges, but either way she seriously doubted whether he would ever put pen to paper.

Her mind raced and raced as her thoughts leapt from Francis to Mrs Flack and back again to Roddy, until eventually in the small hours, she fell into a restless sleep.

At first, when Claire walked out Francis just sat at the kitchen table and cried. He was crying from anger more than anything else. He was furious that Claire dared to patronise

[80]

him, furious that she seemed unable to understand him and his need for sympathy and encouragement and furious that he had broken his glass and that there was no more whisky.

How dared Claire force him to behave in such an undignified way! It was entirely her fault that he had lost his temper. She had driven him to it by her lack of faith in him. Anyone would lose their temper if they were perpetually belittled and patronised and sneered at. Yes sneered at. Claire was definitely sneering when she referred to bridges. What was it she had said?

'You found it *so* difficult to get down to work.' Francis spoke out loud in a ridiculously prissy tone, shaking his head from side to side as he did so. The imitation didn't turn out quite so well as he hoped because his nose was badly blocked from crying. He blew his nose angrily and tried again.

'You found it *so* difficult to get down to work.' That was better. How dared she? Get down to work? He had spent hours on that project about bridges. Thinking about it. Talking about it. You could hardly sit down and write a book without thinking about it first. And he had been quite right to jettison the idea in the long run anyway as there would clearly not have been a market for such a book. Was Claire so stupid that she thought he ought to waste hours, days, perhaps even years of his precious time writing something that no one was ever going to read?

Francis had rarely felt so angry. What he needed was another drink. Perhaps he hadn't looked in the cupboard properly. There might be another bottle of whisky in there somewhere. He stood up and blew his nose again. He had a bloody awful sore throat. He lit a cigarette which made his throat feel even worse and sulkily kicked a piece of broken glass out of the way under the table.

He searched everywhere for some more whisky but there was none to be found and Francis certainly didn't have enough cash on him to go out and buy a bottle. What the hell did Claire mean by just walking out on him like that? If she had been there he wouldn't have needed a drink so badly.

[81]

He'd just been looking forward to a quiet evening watching television and discussing his book about soap operas and then Claire had just walked out on him – for the second time that day. There must have been something the matter with her. Perhaps she was ill. He slammed the door of the bathroom cupboard. There was no whisky in there, either.

The only thing to be done was to go down to the pub and spend whatever cash he could find on having a drink there. There wasn't much point in sitting around all alone in the flat and brooding.

As he walked Francis began to calm down and as he grew calmer he tried to think reasonably about Claire. What, for instance, did she want out of life that she wasn't getting? Nothing, as far as he could see. She had a good job which she liked and she'd got him. And she loved him – or so he had always thought until she'd gone over the top earlier on. Perhaps she was worried about the marriage thing. Well, they'd always agreed about that, hadn't they? And anyway they were planning to decide at Christmas. The trouble was, sometimes it was all right and sometimes it wasn't, but one thing about which Francis was absolutely certain was that they shouldn't marry until they were one hundred percent sure that they were sexually compatible. It was a pity he was getting this damn cold. He was one of those people whose colds tended to last for months. No, Claire couldn't be annoyed about the marriage thing. In any case, she'd say so if she were. They'd always discussed things openly together and besides it was she who knew someone who had only discovered after she was married that her husband was a transvestite. It would be awful if something like that happened to them.

Francis reached the pub and pushed open the swing door. It was pretty crowded inside, but he was glad to be there as the crowd seemed welcoming and he could do with a drink. He sat on a stool by the bar, lit another cigarette, ordered a double whisky and continued to muse about Claire. No, there was nothing he could think of which she might want in life which she didn't have. Oh, of course, she

[82]

might want a bigger and better car or something like that, but he didn't think she really even wanted that. He couldn't imagine what had got into her. She had always been happy before and he knew that temperamentally they were ideally suited. So much so that he sometimes wondered what would happen when he finally got himself established because he would be bound to change a bit then. Become more assertive. More self-confident. Claire might even resent that. She might even become quite jealous when he started to be the major breadwinner. But until now she had always liked caring for him. He knew that, and as he downed his drink he supposed that she would probably be home and repentant the next day.

Just as Francis finished his whisky and was wondering whether he could afford another one, a friend of his came into the pub. A boy he'd known at school and later at university who happened to live round the corner and who worked for a local firm of engineers.

'Hello Francis!'

'Graham. Good to see you.' Francis waved.

Graham came up to the bar.

'What are you drinking?' he asked, putting a friendly hand on Francis's shoulder.

It was pretty lucky, Graham turning up like that to buy Francis a drink, just when Francis was feeling short of change.

Graham sat down on a bar stool which had become conveniently free next to Francis and ordered two double whiskies.

'So what are you doing these days?' he asked.

'I'm working on a history of soap operas.'

Francis and Graham stayed chatting until closing time. Obviously Graham didn't mind paying for Francis's drinks. After all he had a good job.

By the time he staggered home to bed Francis was feeling a great deal more cheerful. In the morning he would probably begin work on his book.

In the morning he changed his mind. He woke with a

[83]

pounding headache, a faint feeling of nausea, an unpleasantly dry mouth and a streaming cold to find Claire
looking down at him with a mug of coffee in her hand.

After falling asleep late Claire had woken early full of
anxiety for Francis. She felt dreadfully guilty about having
left him the evening before. After all the poor fellow was
alone for most of the day with precious little to do, it
seemed a bit tough to abandon him for the night as well. He
might get depressed or something. You could never be
sure. She had never been unemployed and, although she
had seen the ruinous effect it could have on individuals and
their families, perhaps she was lacking in imagination
about how it really felt to wake up day after day to the
realisation that there was nothing which you had to do.
Poor, poor Francis. She must hurry back and see if he was
all right before going to work.

When she reached the flat Claire, in a penitent mood,
made some coffee for Francis and carried it into the
bedroom where he was fast asleep, not, she thought,
altogether surprisingly. She wondered how he had spent
the evening and hoped that he hadn't felt too lonely.

'Francis,' she said gently, 'Francis.'

He opened one bleary eye. God how his head pounded.

'Wake up, I've brought you some coffee, but I can't stay
long or I'll be late for work.' She put the coffee on the
bedside table, bent down and kissed him and then sat on
the bed.

Francis opened his eyes wide.

'Why did you go away like that?' he asked. 'What on
earth was the matter? Just when I wanted to talk about my
new plan.' His throat was agony. 'And I've got a horrid
cold,' he snivelled.

'Poor you,' said Claire, putting her hand on his forehead.
'Drink your coffee, that'll make you feel better. Do you
think you've got a temperature?'

'Probably.'

'Oh dear, is there anything else I can get you before I go to
work, like an aspirin or something?'

[84]

Francis thought he would like a couple of aspirins for his headache. Claire went to fetch them from the bathroom cupboard. When she came back Francis was snuffling and drinking his coffee.

'It's all very well for you,' he said, 'but you never seem to get such bad colds as I do.' He looked up at Claire. She really had a lovely face and he was glad that she had come back to look after him. He put his hand out to take hers. She put her hand in his and sat on the bed again.

'Look,' he said, 'I've got this awful cold, so leave me alone for a bit will you? I mean, don't go on about the Tech and the jewellery-making and all that. Please. When I feel up to it, I'll start my book about soap operas. I was going to start work on it this morning but I can't – not feeling like this.' He took another gulp of his coffee.

'So when do you think you'll be ready to start?' Claire asked with a faint hint of irritation.

'It depends on this cold. My colds sometimes last all winter. Christ, I feel awful.'

'So no more sex till March if the cold lasts all winter,' said Claire tartly. As soon as she spoke, she regretted it. What was the matter with her these days? She was finding it increasingly difficult to control her irritation, but it was rather annoying to see an able-bodied young man lying in bed in mid-October, saying that he had a common cold which was about to last for another five months.

'Well, I must be off,' she said abruptly. 'See you this evening and I hope you'll be feeling better.' And she left the flat.

[85]

CHAPTER VIII

After a busy morning dealing with her paperwork in the office, Claire set out to call on a family she had been looking after for several years. In fact it was one of her more hopeful families, so much so that she thought she might soon be able to close the case.

The Bundys lived in Brontë Buildings and when Claire first knew them, the mother – a single parent – was recovering from a mastectomy, the older son was in prison for rape, the second son was probably peddling drugs, the two daughters were quite out of control and to add to poor Mrs Bundy's troubles, she had a Down's syndrome baby. Claire supposed then that things could hardly get much worse for the Bundys but she did wonder if there was any chance of them getting any better.

As she drove towards the Brontë Buildings, Claire decided that although Mrs Bundy's lot was hardly an enviable one, it had certainly improved over the years. The rapist whom his mother loved was still inside, but the drug pedlar whose threatening behaviour used to terrify Mrs Bundy had gone to Bangkok a couple of years ago and never been seen since. One of the girls had married and gone to live in Manchester and the other girl, deprived of her sister's bad influence, had settled down and found a job and a decent boyfriend and had become a tower of strength, often helping to look after the baby. In addition to all this, Mrs Bundy's brother had moved in with her. Claire wondered if he really was her brother, but in any case, the man seemed honest and hard-working and the atmosphere in the flat had certainly become much happier since his arrival. In fact Mrs Bundy was a changed woman, only weeping occasionally for her rapist son who, she insisted, never done it.

Claire hadn't visited the Bundys for several months, but she felt it was time she looked in just to make sure that everything was all right with the baby and that Mrs Bundy was getting all the help to which she was entitled as a result of the child's handicap. Claire liked the idea of seeing the Bundys. She had grown quite fond of Mrs Bundy over the years and was interested to know how she was getting along and anyway it was a relief to call on families where things seemed to be genuinely improving.

As Claire left Brontë Buildings having found Mrs Bundy in a cheerful mood and satisfied that the family was still more or less all right, she glanced across the road at Thackeray Buildings and thought of Mrs Flack. She couldn't understand why Mrs Flack was so much on her mind. She had visited plenty of families in a worse way than the Flacks – take the Bundys when she first knew them – and had managed not to take her worries home and yet last night she seemed to have been worrying quite as much about the Flacks as she was about Francis or her own brother, Roddy.

Perhaps it was something to do with her not having managed to see the child, Yolande, properly. After all, there had been three telephone calls about that child and the possibility of its being beaten. If it was still being beaten at this moment, it was almost as though it were Claire's fault. As she was so near she might just as well look in again on the off chance of getting a closer look at Yolande. She could easily say that she was just passing by and wondered if Yolande was well enough to go back to school.

[87]

She crossed the road and climbed the gloomy outside staircase to the third floor of Thackeray Buildings. Poor Mrs Flack, she really did need help. It was hardly surprising if she beat her children when she was shut up all day with them in a dreadful place like this. It might help her of course if she could lose a bit of weight. She would feel healthier then, and possibly stronger and marginally more able to cope with life.

As Claire knocked on the door of number thirty-eight, she heard a deep bark from the dog, Barry, who like Nana in *Peter Pan* had probably been left in charge of the children. Claire smiled to herself at the thought of Peter Pan appearing and teaching the grubby little, runny-nosed boy called Trevor how to fly. There was a pause and the dog barked again. No one seemed to be in.

The door of the next door flat opened and the same baleful woman whom Claire had seen the day before looked out rudely for an instant and shut the door again.

Claire decided to knock once more before giving up but there was still no answer, only another husky bark from the dog, so she turned to go down the steps.

Coming up the steps towards her was a good-looking young man whom she instantly recognised as the young man whose minivan had been blocking her way when she left Thackeray Buildings the morning before.

'Morning Miss,' he said as he approached, and then did a double take. 'Seen you some place before, 'aven't I?' He smiled in a friendly fashion.

'Probably around here,' said Claire. 'Actually it might have been you who saw me out of my parking space yesterday morning.' She pointed across the road in the vague direction of where she had been parked.

'Oh yes, I remember,' said the young man, and he smiled and nodded as he went on up the steps.

Claire turned round, vaguely curious as to where he was going and was surprised to see him stop in front of the door to number thirty-eight.

'I don't think there's anyone in,' she called. 'I've been knocking on the door myself.'

'Don't worry,' said the young man. 'This is my place. Was you looking for someone?'

Claire was astounded. 'Are you Gary Flack then?' she asked, walking back up the steps towards him.

'Himself,' said the young man and bowed facetiously.

It struck Claire as perfectly extraordinary that this clean, good-looking cheerful person could be in any way connected with poor, bloated, unhappy Mrs Flack. She had read somewhere that people usually married or lived with other people of roughly the same level of attraction. Paula Yates and Bob Geldof – both very attractive; Neil and Glenys Kinnock about on a par with each other; Prince Andrew and Fergie – absolutely on a par – and among her own friends the same seemed to be more or less true. It was obvious really. Attractive people could afford to be choosy, so they could always find other attractive people. But it was quite impossible to imagine how, even three babies ago and two stone lighter, Mrs Flack could ever have been half as attractive as her husband.

'I was – er – looking for your wife,' said Claire. 'I come from the Social Services. I saw her yesterday, but was a bit worried about the little girl – Yolande is it?' She glanced down at the file in her arms. 'It seems she hasn't been very well.'

'Come on in,' said Gary Flack, opening his front door.

Claire followed Gary into the flat where they were met by Barry padding down the passage towards them.

Gary invited Claire into the sitting room and they both sat down. Gary lit a cigarette. Perched on the edge of his own settee, he looked far more awkward and ill at ease than he had done, walking jauntily in the street.

'Smoke?' he suddenly said, offering the packet to Claire. Claire didn't usually smoke but she occasionally did just to help relax the atmosphere. Besides it seemed friendlier on the whole to accept a cigarette which was offered to you.

A large paw pushed open the door which had been left ajar and Barry came in and lay down in the silence between Gary and Claire.

'Lovely dog,' said Claire, bending forward to pat the giant on the head. 'My dad's got a big dog too. But not as big as Barry.'

'What's he got then?' asked Gary.

'Just a mongrel,' said Claire. Then she sat up smartly, straightened her files on her lap and looked around keenly. 'Children not here?' she asked brightly.

'Alma's taken the kids to her mum's for the night.'

Claire vaguely wondered why Gary had invited her in.

'I didn't see Yolande yesterday – well barely. She was tucked up in bed. Was she any better this morning?' she asked.

Gary Flack had to admit, as he drew on his cigarette, that he hadn't seen Yolande this morning. Things weren't really that good between him and Alma. Hadn't been for a while. He'd looked in yesterday morning just to see the kids and Alma'd told him she'd had enough. She was going over to her mum's for a few days. Often as not these days he slept round at a friend's place. But he couldn't go without seeing his kids. In his opinion kids needed their dad, especially with a mother like Alma. Alma was always having a go at them. Trouble with Alma was she'd let herself go after the little boy was born. Never made anything of herself no more. Claire should have seen her a few years back. Always had her hair done nice. Gary swept his hand over his head to demonstrate the care that Alma used to take with her appearance. Made herself up proper, but she never bothered no more. Gary's mate's wife had two kids but she hadn't let herself go – not the way Alma had. And look at all the weight she'd put on: must've put on at least two stone. Alma always was a big girl, but she was a terrific size now.

Of course things were difficult. Gary, warming to his theme, leaned forward, his elbows resting on his knees.

'I bin out of work, see.'

Claire remembered the ladders on top of Gary's minivan and wondered if he was in work now, or if he was doing a bit of moonlighting. Mrs Flack had certainly implied that her husband was unemployed.

'Help a mate out sometimes, doing a bit of decorating –
nothing much,' said Gary as though he had read Claire's
thoughts. 'Can be hard at times, though,' he went on. 'You
feel guilty if you go for a pint of beer, but that bastard is
allowed to eat us out of house and home.' He pointed at
Barry. 'She won't hear of him going. Eats a pound of meat a
day, but she'll bloody fly at you if you suggest getting rid of
him. Anyway I comes round most days to see the kids – can't
do much more.' Gary looked careworn beyond his years. 'I
dunno what to do,' he said, 'I dunno,' and he put his head in
his hands.

'How long do you think your wife will be staying with her
mother?' Claire had a nasty feeling that Yolande had been
whisked away from under her nose and wouldn't be back
until her bruises had faded.

There was a long pause and then Gary suddenly blurted
out, 'She belts them kids sometimes and I don't think its
right. Not little kids like that. I've told her but she won't
listen. I've even told her that they'll take the kids away from
her if she don't leave off.'

Claire leaned forward sympathetically. Gary, his elbows
on his knees, was holding his head between his hands and
staring hard at the floor.

It crossed Claire's mind that the anonymous man who had
telephoned her office to report that Yolande Flack was being
beaten up might well have been Gary. He was undoubtedly
very upset about the matter. She asked him if he thought
things would be better with the children staying at their
grandmother's.

Gary's mother-in-law was a bit of an old Tartar, he
wouldn't fancy staying at her place for long himself. He gave
a wry smile. But the old girl wouldn't hurt the kids. Wouldn't
hurt a hair on their heads. She'd be fussing over them all day
and to tell the truth they were better off over there with her
than they were alone at home with their mother.

Claire explained that there was very little that she could do
about Yolande or any of the other children for that matter
unless she could see them and then of course, if they really

[91]

were in danger, various steps could be taken. She would give Gary her number at work and perhaps he could give her a ring – he should ask for Claire Potter – and let her know when the children were back at home. She would call round again then and see how things went from there.

It didn't seem much good to be grassing on your own wife. Gary rubbed his hands together and looked awkward. But it was the kids – poor little blighters.

Claire assured him that under no circumstances would she dream of mentioning that he had contacted her and that in any case she wasn't there to cause trouble but to help make things easier for people if she could. Of course Gary was worried about his children and what he was doing was entirely for their benefit, both right and, if he didn't mind her saying so, courageous. He was in a very difficult position – she certainly didn't envy him – and she just hoped that things would soon get sorted out. Gary had mentioned that his wife was very overweight. Claire had to admit that she had noticed that and she wondered if Alma had thought of going to see the doctor who would advise her about a diet. If she could lose a bit of weight it might do her the world of good.

According to Gary, Alma didn't care for doctors and anyway if he ever mentioned her weight she just flew at him.

Poor Gary, Claire felt really sorry for him. He could only be in his early twenties – two or three years younger than herself she supposed – and he seemed to have the problems of the world on his shoulders. She quite admired him in a way. So many of the people she visited, even people with nothing to hide, found it quite impossible to be frank, as if their whole lives were based on fear. Gary Flack was surprisingly frank and yet he clearly didn't find it easy to betray – as he saw it – his wife.

'Well, I'll be on my way,' she said, standing up. 'I'll look forward to hearing from you – and I'll be round again as soon as possible to call on the children.'

Gary stood up and walked to the door with Claire.

[92]

'It's young Yolande,' he said. 'She's the one what gets under her mum's skin. She's a good kid, Yolande.' He opened the front door. 'Thanks for coming, Miss,' he said.

He looked so forlorn standing there talking about young Yolande that it was all Claire could do to restrain herself from leaning forward and patting him comfortingly on the arm.

But she just smiled sweetly and said, 'We'll sort something out,' as he shut the door.

Claire had two more calls which she wanted to do that afternoon and then she planned to look in at the office on her way home. She had been expecting a couple of telephone messages and she thought she would just check if they had come through.

'You look tired,' said Barry, her team leader, as she came back into the office. 'Anything the matter?'

'Oh, no,' said Claire. 'I'm fine.' But she felt rather like crying. She always felt like crying if anyone showed any sympathy towards her.

'Well if there is anything, you know you can always cry on my shoulder.'

'No, it's nothing . . .' There was a catch in her voice. 'Nothing at all. It's just that we live in a pretty awful world. And it's so much worse for some than others.' She smiled wanly and went towards her desk.

'Now you know that you mustn't allow yourself to be got down by these things,' Barry said sensibly. 'If you do, you won't be any help to anybody.'

'Oh, I know, I know,' said Claire. 'Just a bit tired. Had a late night.'

'Get a good night's sleep tonight,' said Barry as he took his anorak down from the coat peg. 'I'm sure you'll feel better in the morning.' He pulled on his anorak and left the office.

Dear Barry, he's always so kind and considerate and caring, Claire thought as she glanced at the telephone messages which had been left for her on her desk.

She was just about to leave for home when the telephone rang. It was for her.

'Roddy! What do you want?' Roddy was all she needed.

[93]

'I hear the law came round asking Mum and Dad for my whereabouts.' He laughed a vulgar laugh. 'Now look here, Claire, love, I wasn't there. That's all there is to it. No way was I in Orchard Close the other evening. No way. It's only the silly bitch's word against mine. No one can prove anything. I told you, just stick to the story. I slept at your place. Right? I suppose Dad imagines I was seen breaking and entering. He always did believe the worst about his son . . .'

'Look here, Roddy,' Claire interrupted the stream, 'I don't know what on earth you're talking about. And I'm not sure I want to.'

'Come on now,' Roddy snarled. 'You wouldn't want to let poor Roddy down, now, would you?'

'To tell you the truth, Roddy, I don't want to have anything to do with your sordid affairs and anyway I'm busy now, so I can't talk.' She put the telephone down angrily. Oh dear, she seemed to be losing all her usual calm these days. But damn Roddy! How dared he make such a nuisance of himself and disrupt everyone's lives so? And how dared he think she was prepared to lie to the police for him. If it was just someone else's word against his, then let him sort it out himself anyway. One day he'd have to learn a nasty lesson and in her present mood she felt that the sooner he learned it the better. What the hell had he been up to? Oh, well, she didn't really care. She would rather worry about Gary Flack.'

'I'll be off now,' she said to the secretary who was just stamping some letters.

'Yes, I'm off now too,' said the secretary. 'I've just got to pop this lot in the post.'

Claire gathered up her things, nodded good-bye to the social worker who was manning the telephone for the evening, and left.

As she put her key in the door of the flat she felt faintly apprehensive. She suddenly realised that probably for the first time since she had met him she was conscious of not really looking forward to seeing Francis. She couldn't face the thought of him moaning about his cold and she really didn't know what to say about the ridiculous soap opera nonsense. Her work was tiring enough emotionally without coming home to more problems, and certainly without Roddy.

Needless to say Francis was still lying in bed, having been there all day. He'd got the television propped up on a chair beside him and an ashtray full of cigarette butts on the bedside table. The room stank of stale cigarettes and stuffiness.

'How are you feeling?' Claire asked as she went to the window and opened it.

'Lousy. And why are you opening the window? Do you want me to get pneumonia?'

'It smells in here and anyway you won't get pneumonia. Would you like a cup of tea?'

Francis did want a cup of tea and he wanted something to eat as well. He was starving. He hadn't had anything to eat all day except for a tin of baked beans which he had heated up for himself at lunchtime.

Claire went into the kitchen. Francis seemed to have made an enormous amount of mess just heating up his beans and making some toast. Claire trod on a piece of glass. Oh God! That was the glass that Francis had broken last night and it was still lying in smithereens all over the floor. She went to get a dustpan and brush. She wished she could just sit down and put up her feet and she wished that someone else would bring her a cup of tea or, even better, a drink. She felt an overwhelming wave of self-pity. She didn't normally feel self-pity and it was an emotion which she loathed in others, but she was just so tired and fed up. She knelt on the floor and brushed up the broken pieces of glass and when she turned to stand up, she saw Francis standing there, wrapped in the duvet. His long white feet on the cork floor looked boney and cold and his toe-nails needed cutting.

'Oh Francis,' she said crossly, 'if you're feeling so ill, just get back to bed. I'll bring you some tea and something to eat in a minute. Just let me clear all this mess up first.'

What the hell was the matter with Claire? She seemed so irritable lately. It was really quite hurtful. Francis was feeling like death and all he wanted was a cup of tea and something to eat. Surely that wasn't asking for much. It wouldn't take Claire long to do that for him. It wasn't as if he were asking for a four-course meal.

'Have you forgotten that I have something very important to discuss with you?' Francis asked, as he turned towards the door.

'What's that?' Claire asked distractedly as she emptied the contents of the dustpan into the bin.

'What's that? What do you mean, "what's that?" My book of course.'

'Look, Francis, please go and get back into bed and I'll bring you some supper and some tea and we can talk then. I've had quite a tiring day and I can't cook and discuss your problems at the same time. I'm sorry.'

Francis went sulkily back to the bedroom. He looked ridiculous from behind with the top of his head just appearing over the bulk of duvet gathered round his shoulders. A few tufty spikes of fair hair were sticking up on end.

'And for God's sake, just empty that ashtray before you get back into bed,' Claire called to the retreating mound of duvet.

Didn't Claire realise how ill Francis was feeling? Surely she could empty the ashtray herself just this once. But for the sake of peace and quiet he tipped the mound of cigarette ends sloppily into the wastepaper basket, spilling half of them on the floor, before sinking back into bed. The news was just starting on Channel Four so he changed channels looking for something more suited to his mood. The news was always depressing. Terry Wogan's smiling face appeared on BBC1. That was better. He always liked *Wogan*.

As Claire made the tea and scrambled eggs, she began to wonder again what on earth she was going to say to Francis about soap operas. She didn't want to provoke another row and yet she could not see how she could possibly take the idea seriously nor how she could pretend to encourage such an obviously hopeless one. She could hear the noise of the television coming from the bedroom and supposed bitterly that Francis would claim to be engaged in research. Then she heard Francis coughing and blowing his nose like a trumpet. And how the hell, she asked herself with an uncharacteristic surge of anger, can you be sexually suited to someone who has a cold for six months at a time? Or suited in any way for that matter? Oh dear, poor Francis. She shouldn't think such mean thoughts. It wasn't his fault he had a cold and he probably felt rotten. She was just tired and she must try to be kinder. Then she turned her thoughts to poor Gary Flack. He had a much worse deal than she did, but in some sort of odd way she felt she could identify with him.

She carried the supper into the bedroom and said with a sweet smile, 'I hope this is what you want. Scrambled eggs on toast?'

She gave Francis his supper first and then sat on the bed with her plate balanced on her knee.

'By the way, Roddy telephoned,' said Francis.

'Oh dear, Roddy's in trouble, I'm afraid – do we really want this on?' Claire was gazing vacantly at the television set where Terry Wogan was interviewing a wraithlike actress with a mane of golden hair and she stretched out her hand to turn it off.

'No, don't turn it off for a moment,' said Francis. 'I know her. She's been in *Dallas* or *Dynasty* I'm sure. I can't remember which. Let's just see what she says.'

'So what are your plans for the immediate future?' Terry Wogan asked the actress.

'Well, Terry,' the actress replied, 'I've decided to try my hand at writing and right now I'm working on a history of the soap opera . . .'

CHAPTER IX

The night before she married George, Nancy lay in bed wondering whether she would dare call the whole thing off in the morning. But she knew in her heart of hearts that she wouldn't and neither was she sure that she really wanted to. It would be so cruel to George who did love her, she thought, in an undemonstrative, English sort of way. She knew that she wasn't in love with him but she felt that she would probably never fall in love again in the way that she had with Gregory. But she was fond of George. Even very fond of him and he was kind and thoughtful and generous and she would be able to have children. She longed for children.

She looked at the pale shadow of her white *broderie anglaise* dress hanging outside the cupboard ready for the great day and thought that at least life with George represented change and a brighter outlook for the future. He had applied for a change of job and they were to move away from Bromley to Tonbridge where they had found a moderately priced cottage on which George had been able to make a down payment and of which they would take possession as soon as they returned from their week's honeymoon in Scotland. Nancy was glad to be getting away from Bromley and the future to her seemed full of hope.

And indeed George and Nancy soon settled happily in Tonbridge where they quickly made a few friends and where some eighteen months later their son, Roddy, was born.

Nancy was delighted with Roddy who was clearly the most beautiful baby in the world. He was healthy and bonny and bright. He sat up and crawled before other babies of his age and produced his first tooth at four months. He didn't disturb his parents at night and could walk by the time he was one. Roddy, Nancy felt, must be the envy of all the other young mothers she knew. She and George daydreamed about his future, imagining always greater things for him. He was so clever that he might become a mathematician or an architect. You only had to see the way he played with his bricks.

Nancy was never bored looking after Roddy on whom she doted, in fact, she had never been happier in her life. George continued to be kind and considerate and generous, and was, in addition, hard working and helpful around the house, always ready to mend a fuse or change a washer. He was clever too. Nancy could never understand the clues in the *Times* crossword, but George was brilliant at it and never ceased to surprise her with his general knowledge. Perhaps it wasn't all that surprising, seeing how much he read.

One day in early spring George was standing on a ladder pruning a rose which grew up the side of the house when he slipped and fell to the ground breaking his arm as he landed. His arm had to be in plaster for some six weeks which was a great nuisance, particularly at that time of year when there was so much to be done in the garden. Luckily he had a kind neighbour who offered to help them out.

'Just give us a tinkle if there's anything I can do to help,' Bill said to Nancy. And after that Bill seemed to be forever round at the Potters' house.

Bill was a man in his late thirties who worked for a local newspaper and who seemed to keep rather odd office hours. He had a tired face and a quiet voice and remarkably blue eyes and his wife had just left him so Nancy supposed that he must be rather lonely – he certainly spent enough time drinking coffee with Nancy and pouring his heart out to her between showing her how to prune the roses and putting up shelves for her in the kitchen.

But Nancy was not so naive as to be unaware of the fact that Bill found her attractive. Not that he ever behaved improperly towards her, but it was just perfectly obvious and she was flattered to the point of becoming marginally flirtatious.

Bill began to be more and more of a feature in Nancy's life. So much so that she wondered what would happen when George had the plaster removed from his arm and what excuse Bill would find then for calling. Nancy liked seeing Bill and positively looked forward to his turning up, so much so that if twenty-four hours went by without her seeing him, she felt that the day had somehow been disappointing. She thought of him more and more often. But there could hardly be any harm in that. Then she began idly to daydream about having an affair with him. Of course she would never do such a thing but there was something rather thrilling and tempting about the idea. He was, she thought, really quite attractive with his quiet voice and bright blue eyes and tired face.

After about three or four weeks Nancy realised that she spent most of her day thinking about nothing but Bill so that even Roddy seemed to have taken second place.

'I wonder what time Uncle Bill will come and see us today,' she would say to eighteen-month-old Roddy. Or, 'I think I'll make a pot of tea just in case Uncle Bill looks in'; and, 'Hasn't Uncle Bill put the shelves up nicely?'

Then one day Bill was sitting at her kitchen table having a cup of tea in the middle of the afternoon and the telephone rang. Nancy jumped to her feet to answer it and tripped over a rattle left on the floor by the baby. If Bill hadn't swivelled round in his chair and stretched out his arms to break her fall she would have landed flat on her face on the stone flags. Instead she landed in Bill's arms with the telephone still ringing furiously in her ears. Bill's proximity and the smell of his body sent a thrill of excitement and sheer pleasure through her, but she disentangled herself with a funny smile and made another dash for the telephone.

As she put out her hand to answer it she admitted to herself for the first time that she was in love with Bill and had been for a little while.

The telephone call was from the local electricity board to say when they would be calling to fix the faulty hot plate on her cooker.

'Yes, that will be perfectly all right,' she said. 'Thank you very much. Good-bye.' But in her emotion she did not take in a word of what was said to her and so when the electrician called the next afternoon, she had taken Roddy out in his pram to the shops and she had to wait another ten days before her cooker was mended.

Once Nancy had admitted to herself that she was in love with Bill she spent all her time thinking about whether or not to have an affair with him. She felt sure that he was only waiting for a sign of encouragement from her but she dared not really give one. She would be betraying George in a way which she believed to be truly unacceptable and yet he need never know. Roddy couldn't talk and so could not even tell his father quite often Bill had called over the last few weeks. If George didn't know, Nancy argued to herself, then how could it affect him?

Then there was the major problem of where it would all lead. She had no idea and she was quite frightened of embarking on a passionate love affair. And of course she remembered Gregory and the awful aftermath of that short-lived affair. She didn't want to go through that again – and yet the whole idea was so tempting and so exciting.

George came back from work one evening and announced that he had a few days off. Why didn't they take advantage of it and go away? They could stay with his parents – his mother was always delighted to look after

Roddy – see a few friends and perhaps go up to London to see a play.

The last thing Nancy wanted to do was to go away. She would miss Bill dreadfully, but then perhaps the break would give her a chance to think clearly about what she should do. Apart from that she realised that she would have to go as she had absolutely no excuse for not going and in any case it would be very unkind to George who was not only obviously delighted with the idea from his own point of view, but who clearly thought that it would be a treat for Nancy to go away.

So away they went, and Nancy pined dreadfully for Bill, and George's mother said to George:

'Is Nancy all right? Are you sure you're looking after her properly? She seems awfully quiet – not quite her usual self.' Privately she wondered whether Nancy was not 'expecting' again.

George's sister, Heather, was also quite worried about her old friend and tried questioning her about her private life.

Nancy merely replied that she was blissfully happy. She had never been happier in her life. Who could be unhappy with a wonderful person like George and with a beautiful baby like Roddy? And then she went back to thinking about Bill and his blue eyes and the smell of his body and his quiet voice and how she would let him silently in through the back door – and Roddy would be asleep in his pram – and she would lead him upstairs to the bedroom – but there her own imaginings failed her for she could hardly betray George in his own bed . . . Perhaps she could go to Bill's house, but then she would have to take the baby with her and that was hardly very romantic. So then she went back to thinking about Bill's blue eyes and his quiet voice, and she counted the days and even the hours until she could see him again.

When she got home she found that in fact she was pregnant again and the discovery somewhat changed her attitude. The idea of starting an affair with another man when she was pregnant with George's baby seemed rather horrible and she began to feel ashamed of the thoughts she had entertained, and, although there was no doubt that she was in love with Bill, she began to feel an immense warmth for George whenever she looked at him. He was so kind, with his long face and horn-rimmed spectacles, and so utterly delighted by the thought of the new baby. How could she be so ungrateful to him?

And yet she still pined for Bill who, for some unaccountable reason, had taken to visiting less frequently. Perhaps, having failed to receive a sign of encouragement, he had decided that it would be better to stay away for a while.

A couple of months later, by the time it became general knowledge that Nancy was pregnant, a distance had grown up between her and Bill so that the old carefree feeling of familiarity would have been hard, if not impossible, to recapture. As her pregnancy advanced, Bill distanced himself more and more, and one day George said:

'It's a funny thing about old Bill. We hardly ever seem to see him these days. Do you think we have done something to offend him?'

'Oh, no,' said Nancy. 'How could we have done? I expect he's found a new girlfriend or something.' She felt a violent pang of jealousy as she spoke and then that old, familiar nagging feeling of guilt reared its ugly head. And yet why should she feel guilty? Nothing had been lost – except Bill – and George, thank God, could hardly understand that, nor read her mind, nor dream of what had gone on inside her head, nor know that even as she sat smiling sweetly and knitting bootees for the unborn child, her whole being ached for Bill.

Nancy went on thinking about Bill for a long time after that but she saw him less and less frequently until, at about the time Claire was born, he moved away to another job in another part of the country after which her passion gradually died a natural death, although years later she would occasionally cast her mind back to that strange time and smile to herself and think briefly about what might have been.

[103]

Nancy's mother came to stay for a few days to help when Claire was born. Nancy found it quite refreshing seeing her mother away from the dominating presence of Mrs Larders, particularly as grandchildren seemed to have had a good effect on her, shaking her slightly out of her usual torpor and giving her a long overdue, renewed interest in life. But she could not stay for long as Mrs Larders herself, who was not so young, was quite unwell and Nancy's mother didn't care to leave her alone for many days.

Not long after that Mrs Larders had a stroke and was taken to hospital where after two weeks, she had another stroke and died.

Although shocked by the death of her grandmother with whom she had lived for nearly as long as she could remember, Nancy didn't feel true sorrow. It was almost as if a great lowering cloud had been blown away by a strong wind so that Nancy could at last breathe freely and she was amazed by a strange feeling of liberty and independence about which she kept very quiet since it appalled her and aroused in her all sorts of feelings of guilt.

George decided at around this time that he would like to move back nearer to London, partly to be close to his own family, but now that his mother-in-law was alone it would be nice to be closer to her too. So he applied for a transfer to another branch of the bank and within a few months he and Nancy moved to the mock-Elizabethan house in the suburb where they were to spend the rest of their lives.

With two children to look after, Nancy found that she was permanently busy, especially as Roddy had become quite a handful. Having been the most perfect baby, he had turned into the naughtiest little boy. Nancy had absolutely no idea how to discipline him. She was still as firmly convinced as ever that her children should be brought up free from the haunting guilt which bedevilled her life and which she believed had been instilled in her by her upbringing. Yet how could she discipline the child at all without instilling some sort of conscience? And where was the fine line that divided the conscience proper from pointless guilt? Nancy used to worry a lot about the problem as she reasoned patiently with her little son.

But neither reason, nor George's more heavy handed, old-fashioned form of chastisement of which Nancy strongly disapproved, appeared to have any effect on Roddy who was continually disobedient, destructive, aggressive and bad tempered. Nancy was still convinced that Roddy was very clever and so she decided that all his problems stemmed from the fact that he was bored. Once he went to kindergarten, she was sure that he would change. His mind would be occupied and when he got home he would be tired and less ready for a fight.

So when the time came for Roddy to go to school, Nancy was delighted. She quite looked forward to having only quiet, obedient, cheerful little Claire to look after during the day.

In fact kindergarten didn't solve the problem. The kindergarten teacher complained that Roddy was the most disruptive five year old in the class and he was often quite unpleasant to the other children. The teacher asked Nancy to come and see her to discuss the problem. Was there something at home which was upsetting the child?

Nancy didn't think so. But she was worried and asked herself repeatedly where she was going wrong.

George's attitude was that little boys were always naughty and that the schoolmistress couldn't be very good at her job if she was unable to control a five year old. All Roddy needed was a firm hand and the occasional smack.

After he went to school Roddy became even more impossible at home. Until then he had mildly tolerated his little sister but it was as though he was jealous of her staying at home all day with his mother while he was away and so when he came back from school in the afternoon, he immediately began to persecute her by pinching her, pulling her hair and snatching her toys.

Nancy tried pulling his hair in return and taking away his toys, but nothing seemed to have any effect and he would start taunting his sister again immediately.

'Well,' said Nancy out loud to herself, as Roddy snatched yet another toy from the wailing Claire, 'nothing on earth will ever make him feel guilty. That's something.' It didn't occur to her that as he grew older he might fail to develop a normal conscience. She even thought sometimes that she might be wrong about her upbringing and that perhaps people were either born with or without a sense of guilt.

George could see no problem. As far as he was concerned, Roddy's naughtiness was entirely attributable to Original Sin.

Nancy wasn't sure that she totally approved of the notion of Original Sin. She had long since given up going to church with George and she was firmly convinced that organised religion was responsible for a great deal of unnecessary guilt. Not that George seemed particularly riddled by guilt. But then you never knew what went on in other people's minds.

Sometimes Nancy thought that despite all the books he read and despite his religious fervour, nothing much went on in George's mind. He seemed to accept with unquestioning innocence everything he read and the Christmas Story as well.

By the time Roddy was eight his behaviour had not improved at all, if anything it had become even worse and was a great cause of anxiety to both Nancy and George. There was no doubt about it that Roddy was a problem child who despite his parents' confidence in his intelligence, refused to learn anything at school and who persistently bullied and provoked his sister. He was light-fingered, egocentric and deceitful and yet at times he could be incredibly charming. He was good-looking and when the occasion merited, he could produce a broad and winning smile.

He wound his mother round his little finger partly because Nancy, who loved her son, desperately wanted to believe the best of him, so that when he explained, for instance, that he had found the pound in his pocket in the gutter on his way home from school, Nancy believed him because she wanted to.

[106]

The Sixties were in full swing and Nancy was considerably influenced by the mood of the times, especially where the progressive upbringing of children was concerned. She eagerly read and re-read the works of Dr Spock, anxious for some guidance about how to deal with her difficult son.

Claire, on the other hand, was no problem at all. In fact she was an ideal child, sunny, bright, easy and friendly. She even managed to put up with her brother's taunting with amazing equanimity. She had a pet hamster which she tended with loving care and whose cage door Roddy frequently left open by mistake on purpose and she had a kitten which she never forgot to feed.

Nancy treated Claire exactly as she treated Roddy, but with entirely different results. Neither child was made to eat anything he or she disliked and nor did they have to come to meals at regular times, they went to bed when they liked and wore what they liked and were never punished, by Nancy at least.

George, who was mildly annoyed by Nancy's attitude, adopted a more traditional way of dealing with his children, particularly his son.

Neither child was sent away to school but both were educated locally in private day schools. Claire did quite well at school and was popular with the teachers as well as her peers, whereas Roddy was permanently under threat of expulsion and seemed quite unable to apply himself to pass any exams. The older he grew, the more anxious his parents became and the less they liked his friends. He always seemed to pick up the most dicey characters – sly, rowdy, sneering, dirty-minded boys and later, silly, flighty, selfish little girls.

But Nancy never despaired. She loved Roddy and was sure that he, with his disarming smile and easy talk, loved his parents. All this love, she felt, must eventually stand him in good stead and he would eventually grow up and turn into a satisfactory member of society. Even do great things. After all, Winston Churchill had never passed an exam. Winston Churchill's failure to pass any exams must have provided a constant source of comfort to anxious parents over the years. Even more so than the combined works of Dr Spock.

So whenever some change took place in Roddy's life – when he moved up a form, or changed teachers, or started to learn a new subject, or dropped an old one, Nancy firmly believed that things would start to improve and that at last he would learn to harness his talents.

One day when Roddy was about twelve, Nancy was washing something in the kitchen sink and vaguely glancing out of the window at the garden when she saw the gate swing open and Roddy come strolling up the path, dragging his satchel along the ground behind him. She wished he wouldn't do that. As he passed by a bed of tulips which were just bursting into magnificent flower and which Nancy had been watching over the weeks with delight, he paused and looked at them.

Nancy particularly treasured the flowerbed outside the kitchen window because it cheered her thoughout the year as she washed up or peeled potatoes and brought her joy as she did her daily chores.

She often mentioned her special flowerbed and talked of what she was going to put in it for the early spring or the autumn and it was inconceivable that Roddy was unaware of her love for it. As she watched him drop his satchel and systematically break the opening buds from their stems, Nancy momentarily froze. Even Roddy could not be so wilfully malicious.

And then she felt a swelling surge of violent anger well up inside her. She dropped what she was holding and ran to the garden where she grabbed the unsuspecting Roddy by the shoulders and shook him and shook him shouting as she did so.

'You horrible, horrible little boy,' she shouted as she tightened her grip on his upper arms, 'spiteful, evil, hateful, you never do anything right – you'll break your parents' hearts in the end – as it is you've never done anything but be a disappointment from the word go – get out of my sight –' she released her hold and gave him a great push so that he fell over in the bed of ruined tulips.

Nancy turned and ran into the house, tears streaming down her face. She had never dreamed that she would ever speak to one of her children like that. In fact she couldn't remember when she had last lost her temper. Probably when she was a child. She had done a dreadful and wicked thing. Roddy had harmed the tulips, but she had harmed Roddy. Who could be expected to have faith in the child if his own mother didn't? How could she have said those dreadful things to him?

Whenever anything went wrong with Roddy after that, she felt that she was partly to blame because of what she had said on that traumatic afternoon. A disappointment from the word go.

CHAPTER X

Claire heard no more from Roddy for a while, which was just as well as she had plenty of other problems to deal with. There was Francis, still moaning about his cold, snuffling and spluttering around the flat, and overflowing with self-pity now that the kibosh had been put on his soap opera plan. That was just as well too, but all the same it left Francis as aimless, if not even more so, than before. Claire no longer mentioned the Tech nor the jewellery-making course. It was obvious that Francis had no intention of doing anything about that and so it would be better to think of something else. But what?

Sometimes Claire thought that Francis should just go round to the Job Centre and sign on for some sort of labouring job.

Francis, on the other hand, maintained that his asthma made it quite impossible for him to take on a labouring job which was a shame really because he quite fancied the idea.

As far as Claire could see Francis had really reached some sort of a dead end. And even their relationship which she had always believed to be rock solid seemed to be running into trouble.

Of course she knew that all couples had their ups and downs and she hoped things would begin to straighten themselves out again soon, but something which really troubled her and which had been niggling at her for two or three weeks now was that the relationship had suffered a basic change which dated from the moment or, at any rate, crystallised at the moment when she was on her knees brushing up some broken glass from under the table and when she turned and looked at Francis's feet.

Claire accepted quite calmly the fact that someone you loved could be intensely irritating. Their attitudes, their opinions, the mess they left in the kitchen or the bathroom, even the way they ate could be infuriating at times yet you went on loving them and looking forward to seeing them and wanting to be with them. But what she could not accept was that you could profoundly dislike a part of somebody's body and still love that person. Yet as she had turned with her dustpan in her hand and looked at Francis's boney feet with their uncut toenails, she had disliked them intensely. Did this mean that she no longer loved Francis?

She cast her mind back to their recent holiday in Italy and remembered how happy they had been then. Could everything really have changed so quickly? The more she thought about Francis, the more anxious she became and the more she came to dread the future. Until now she had not questioned the idea of spending the rest of her life with Francis, but it was as though one small question – about his feet – had opened the floodgates for all sorts of doubts to come rushing through.

At work Claire was distracted and nervous and at home she continued to be unusually irritable and, Francis thought, rather cold. He could not for the life of him imagine what he had done wrong.

One morning Claire left early for work in a particularly snappy mood. She was expecting an important telephone call from someone called Frick or Fluck or something equally ridiculous – something to do with a battered baby. Francis wished that she would spare less concern for battered babies and a little more for him.

He still had his cold and was coughing a lot and he hadn't yet decided what to do with his life which was, after all,

[111]

quite an important consideration. It was a real shame about the soap opera thing. It had been quite a shock at the time when he heard that actress talking to Wogan, so much so in fact that it had brought on an attack of asthma which was particularly disagreeable on top of a cold. Claire had actually been quite sympathetic at the time, he had to admit, but she certainly hadn't shown much more sympathy since. He bloody well hoped she was being nicer to the Flicks and Flucks of this world that she was to him or they wouldn't be very grateful to our wonderful social services.

Francis was lying in bed with his hands behind his head. It was quite cold in the bedroom, so he didn't think he'd get out yet to fetch the television. Anyway, he had some thinking to do.

He just had to work out what had gone wrong with his relationship with Claire. Nothing about their life was any different to what it had always been and she had been perfectly happy up till now. She had stopped going on at him about the Tech, so she couldn't be annoyed about that. Perhaps it was just that she was worried about Roddy, but then he didn't see why she should take out her anxieties about Roddy on him. He leaned over to the bedside table and took a cigarette and lit it. The worst of it all was that if he asked her what the matter was, she either pretended not to hear or said 'nothing'.

It couldn't really be sex that was worrying her either – after all it had been fine when they were on holiday and no one in their right mind could expect great passion from a man with a bloody awful cold. For Christ's sake, that would be asking too much! If she had a cold she probably wouldn't be feeling like it either. No Claire had never been that unreasonable. Anyway his cold wasn't likely to last forever.

The more he thought, the more puzzled he became.

He stubbed out his cigarette in the ashtray beside the bed and looked at his watch. It was just after ten. He wondered how to spend the rest of the day and vaguely thought that he might get up, make the bed, tidy up the flat, go out and buy something nice for supper, perhaps even a bottle of wine to welcome Claire back with in the evening. If that didn't put her in a good mood, then he'd just have to despair.

He heaved himself out of bed and pulled on his clothes. His Aran-knit jersey was a bit grubby but it would have to do for a few more days. He didn't feel like going to the launderette and sitting around there with a cold. Besides you didn't want to go giving your cold to other people.

It took him about an hour to tidy the flat and when he had done it he looked around proudly. Claire would be very pleased when she came in. At the thought of Claire being pleased with him, he cheered up. He was going to buy two steaks and a bottle of wine and lay the table before she got back and then everything would be fine again. He was sure of it.

On the way to the shops Francis passed the Bricklayers Arms. He glanced at his watch as he reached the door. It was getting on for midday. He might as well just pop in and have a pint and a sandwich. Save him troubling about lunch.

When Francis came out of the pub a couple of hours later and as he walked on in the direction of the shops, he suddenly realised that he didn't have enough money left to buy a bottle of wine as well as the steaks. Come to that, he wasn't sure he had enough even for the steaks. Oh well, what a shame. Never mind, he'd tidied the flat – Claire would be pleased enough about that. He'd get the steak and wine another day.

He strolled on down the road wondering how to fill the rest of the afternoon and stopped in front of the Job Centre, vaguely staring in through the window and then, on a sudden impulse, went inside. Usually he avoided the Job Centre like the plague. They never had anything suitable for people like him. But perhaps he could just tell Claire that he had actually been there then she would have no excuse for going on at him about having nothing to do. He spent some time reading the notices pinned up on the boards and of course, he was quite right – there was nothing interesting

[113]

there at all. A few labouring jobs which obviously wouldn't do, and then there was a barman needed for three nights a week in a local pub. There was no point in that. Otherwise there were some clerical jobs and a dentist's assistant was needed. Well, he would tell Claire that he'd tried.

When he came out of the Job Centre he thought he'd go back to the flat because the damp weather was making his cough worse and on his way he passed a small grocer's shop kept by some Indians. He went in to buy some matches, having left his own in the pub and, as he came out he was struck by the buckets full of cut flowers which the Indians were displaying on the pavement outside the shop. They really were quite pretty. Perhaps he would buy a small bunch for Claire. He felt in his pocket for his change and brought out a handful of coins which he stared at quizzically in the palm of his hand. Yes he could just manage it. He pulled a few dripping brown chrysanthemums from one of the buckets and carried them back into the shop to pay for them.

He felt rather silly as he walked on home carrying the flowers awkwardly clasped in his hand. He hoped he wouldn't meet anyone he knew.

When he reached the flat he couldn't find a flower vase or anything else suitable to put them in. Eventually, in despair, he emptied the contents of a half full Nescafé jar into a saucepan and put the flowers in that on the kitchen table. They looked rather pathetic, those four chrysanthemums, stuck in that jar on the table and anyway they seemed to be dropping some of their petals already. Claire probably wouldn't mind as she liked flowers. He just hoped that she'd be in a better frame of mind than she had been lately when she got home after work.

Claire had gone off to work in a dither that morning. The afternoon before Gary Flack had telephoned while she was out and had been told to ring again in the morning. She hoped he would and presumed that that meant that the children and their mother were now back in Thackeray Buildings. She had been beginning to wonder whether

Gary would in fact ring and had called round on one occasion to check that the flat was still empty, which it was.

She had only been in her office for about five minutes when the telephone rang and, sure enough, it was for her, and sure enough it was Gary.

'Alma's still over her mum's place,' he said down the telephone. 'But I'd like to see you, Miss, if I could.'

Of course Claire would see Gary. She would be delighted to help in any way she could. She could come round to Thackeray Buildings that morning if it suited him.

But, Gary was a bit embarrassed, he would rather meet her some other place if she didn't mind. A lot of people in Thackeray Buildings had nothing better to do than to mind everybody else's bleedin' business.

Claire quite understood that and arranged to meet Gary in a café within walking distance of her office. By the time she got there Gary was already sitting at a table with a cup of tea in front of him. He jumped up when he saw her and smiled warmly. Could he get her a cup of tea or coffee or something? She glanced at his rather grey tea in a thick white cup and said she'd have the same, and Gary went to the counter to fetch it. As he sat down again she put her hand out towards him with the money for the tea and for an instant she thought he looked faintly offended. He might be on the dole, but he could afford a bleedin' cup of tea.

She thanked him and put her money back in her purse.

Gary piled three teaspoonfuls of sugar into his cup and began to stir his tea vigorously.

He hadn't phoned Claire before because Alma and the kids were still over at Alma's mother's place. And to be honest he didn't know when they'd get back. He'd been over to see them last week – taken the dog and left him there – and the kids seemed all right. Well Alma wasn't likely to beat them up – not with her mum around, he didn't think so anyway – so he should be pleased that they were there – but the trouble was he'd tried calling again yesterday and Alma's mum had refused to let him in. It could be that Alma had had a go at the kids and her mum was protecting her or it could be that Alma had put her mum against him. That wouldn't have been very difficult because her mum had never had much time for him. Not since he got Alma in the club. They was only kids then but Claire should have heard the names Alma's mum called him. He'd never heard such language from someone who called herself a lady and gave herself such bleedin' airs. Gary's mum would never have talked to anyone like that and she didn't give herself airs – she was just an ordinary working woman – well, so was Alma's mum for all her airs.

'What happened when you called, then?' Claire asked.

Gary had rung the doorbell and waited for a bit, then the lace curtains twitched and he saw the cow peeping out to see who was there. He'd waited a bit longer and no one answered the door, so he rang again and waited. Still she didn't open the bleedin' door, so he began knocking with his fists and shouting a bit. Nothing nasty, just making a bit of a din so's she'd come to the door. He knew her type. She probably only opened the door because she was frightened of what the neighbours would think.

Claire should've heard the old bag. Dreadful language she'd used to him, telling him never to show his face again, blinding and bleeding like nobody's business. Must've put the neighbours' ears out on stalks. When he'd said he'd only come to see his kids she'd gone wild. Nobody would let him see them poor kids, not after the way he'd treated them. Black and blue all over they were and if he so much as dared to show his face again she'd call the police and get the welfare on him. And then she started on about women, accusing him of every sort of thing and yelling her head off all the time. In the end he couldn't take no more and he could see there was no chance of getting so much as a bloomin' toe through the front door so he'd just turned round and walked away, leaving the old bag there hollering on her front doorstep.

As far as Claire could see, Alma must have told her mother that the bruises on Yolande's body had been inflicted by Gary which made things pretty difficult since it all boiled down to being a case of his word against hers unless there was an outside witness, which seemed unlikely.

'Only Yolande,' said Gary. 'And we don't want to go dragging the poor kid into it.'

'Well the child's involved whether she likes it or not,' said Claire and she might well confide in a social worker, if only a social worker could get to see her. If they didn't come back soon perhaps Claire could get in touch with the social services for the area where they were. Apart from anything else the child ought to be going to school and there would most likely be trouble about that before long.

Gary was made very, very angry by the suggestion that he had beaten up his children. He wasn't the violent sort. Would never lay a finger on one of his own kids. The mistake he'd made was not to give his name when he'd rung the welfare in the first place.

So it was him.

But he'd been scared of trouble. He didn't want no more trouble than what he'd already got.

Claire looked at Gary. He had a nice face, a really nice face and a frank smile. She was absolutely certain that he was telling the truth.

For a moment Gary caught her eye and then turned his head away and dragged nervously at his cigarette.

'Look,' said Claire, 'try not to worry about it too much. As soon as I get back to the office I'll get in touch with the people over there, and I'll get a social worker to go round and call on your mother-in-law.'

Gary doubted that anyone would have any more success than he'd had getting into the house. But he supposed it was worth a try. He smiled at Claire who was looking at him with an expression of real concern. The funny thing was that Gary had never really had anything much to do with Claire's type before and he always imagined rich people had no heart.

'I wish I *were* rich,' Claire laughed, and blushed slightly. 'Anyway,' she added, 'I expect some do and some don't.' She pushed aside her empty tea cup and stood up. She had to be getting back to her office.

[117]

Gary said he'd better be going too. He wanted to drop round and see his mate who might have a job for him.

'I shouldn't have said that, should I?' he said with a grin as he opened the door of the café for her.

'Heavens!' said Claire, 'you've got enough troubles on your plate – I'm not going to bother about a spot of moonlighting. But don't tell anyone I said so.' She began to walk along the pavement with Gary at her side.

'My van's parked along here,' he said, 'like a ride?'

Claire didn't really know what made her accept, as it was only a five-minute walk back to her office, but she climbed into the van beside Gary.

'I sometimes wish my boyfriend would do something like that. He's on the dole too, you see,' she said.

'Sorry, Miss,' Gary turned his head to look at her suddenly, 'I didn't think of you having problems too.'

'I'm called Claire – and – don't worry, I shouldn't really have mentioned it.' She had absolutely no business to be discussing Francis with Gary. She couldn't imagine what had got into her. 'It's left down here,' she said, and pointed down a side road.

As Gary drew up outside her office, she added,

'Now keep in touch won't you? I want to be able to let you know how things go. Thanks for the lift – and the tea – and good-bye for now.' This time she touched him lightly on the shoulder before getting out of the van.

'There you go then, Claire,' said Gary, leaning over to pull the door shut after her. Then with a cheery wave and a spurt of acceleration he was gone, leaving Claire standing on the pavement feeling somewhat dazed.

She stared vacantly at the back of the minivan as it sped away down the street, sighed and shook her head as though to rid her mind of confusion. If she began to fall for Gary, then life would become unbearably complicated.

She turned and walked into the building where her office was and up the stairs to the first floor. She really wished that Francis would stir his stumps. He hadn't half so much to put up with as Gary had and yet all he could do was to lie in bed watching television and feeling sorry for himself. She began to wonder if Francis even really cared for her. He certainly didn't care in anything like the way Gary cared for his children. In fact when she came to think about it, Francis was quite a selfish person. It was odd that she had never thought of him in that light before, perhaps because she had been concentrating on trying to encourage him all the time. Well that didn't seem to have done him much good.

For the rest of the morning she sat at her desk only half concentrating on her papers, mostly absorbed with thoughts of Gary or Francis, or both. But she did manage to get in touch with someone to go and call on Alma Flack at her mother's house. Gary had given her the address but she warned the social worker in question that she might have trouble gaining access.

Claire could hardly imagine Gary Flack lounging around all day, propping up bars and feeling that life had treated him badly, which indeed it had, she was thinking, as she parked her car in the street outside her flat that evening. Gary Flack was full of life, fighting for his children, finding jobs wherever he could and even the way he moved and drove his car reflected an inner energy. When Claire got upstairs she would find Francis doing nothing and having done nothing all day. No wonder he was so sorry for himself. He must be bored out of his mind.

As Claire walked into the flat she heard the usual noise of the television coming from the sitting room.

'Hello,' she called, 'I'm back,' and banged the door to behind her.

As she did so Francis came bounding out of the sitting room with an unusually perky air and kissed her warmly.

'Come on in,' he said. 'I've been to the Job Centre and I've bought you some flowers and I've tidied up the flat. Look . . .' He waved his arms around as they walked into the kitchen.

As she saw the four brown chrysanthemums limply standing in the Nescafé jar, Claire burst out laughing.

'Couldn't you find anything better to put them in?' she asked, but she gave him a big kiss and felt deeply touched.

Poor Francis. She had been having such mean thoughts about him all day and here he had being really trying to please her. The flat was amazingly clean and tidy and – most surprising of all – he had even been to the Job Centre. What was more, he looked quite pleased with himself as a result of his efforts. But of course there had been nothing doing at the Job Centre. Never mind – it was always worth looking. One day he might be lucky.

Claire looked at Francis as he pranced around the kitchen, so pleased with himself, and felt a wave of irritation tempered with pity, and at the same time a nagging intrusive guilt. Why had he suddenly begun to irritate her so much and what on earth was she to do about it? Those chrysanthemums were ridiculous stuck in that Nescafé jar and although she had been touched by them when she first saw them, they had now begun to annoy her.

Those chrysanthemums dropping their brown petals on the kitchen table reminded Claire of suspension bridges and unwritten books and unattended courses and of failed degrees . . . Oh dear, she felt so nasty . . . poor, poor Francis . . . She must remember that he had had a horrid childhood and that it was hardly his fault that he was a chronic asthmatic. She must always remember that and try to be kind and patient. And she must always remember how he needed her.

Suddenly she had a vision of herself, twenty years hence, still living with Francis, a disillusioned, disappointed middle-aged man. What would he be like then? Most disillusioned middle-aged people were tempted to take to the bottle. Oh poor Francis. She had never thought of him in those terms before. In fact she had always seen him as someone who would eventually find a path and who, having found his path, would succeed.

What had made her so confident? And why was her attitude suddenly changing so radically?

Francis started to cough, and he went on coughing for what seemed like an eternity.

'Bloody cold,' he said when he finally stopped, 'can't get rid of it.'

For supper they heated up some frozen pizzas which Claire had bought on her way home from work.

Claire was quite cheerful although she felt far from cheerful. She thought she should make an effort as, after all, Francis had made some kind of an effort himself, however feeble.

Francis was cheerful too. He was so happy that Claire was in such a relaxed mood again at last. Perhaps it had something to do with the chrysanthemums and his having tidied up the flat. He was really glad he'd done that for her. Poor Claire, she probably got tired at times what with listening to all those people's dreadful problems every day. He'd try to make a bit of an effort for her more often.

Later that night Claire rebuffed Francis's advances. She felt tired – and how could she make love to someone she pitied in the way she now pitied Francis? And how dared he think that with four wilting chrysanthemums he had bought the right to screw her? Oh God! Then, as she turned over to settle for the night, she began to think about Gary's robust male frame and his self-respecting walk until just as she finally drifted off to sleep, two large tears rolled down her cheeks onto the pillow.

CHAPTER XI

The next day Francis and Claire were invited out for supper with some friends. Claire was glad because they hadn't been out much lately so it would be a welcome change and anyway she thought it would do them both good to be with other people the way things were at the moment.

When she got back from work she went to have a bath and as she lay in the warm water vaguely wondering what to wear she heard the door bell ringing. Who on earth could that be? Roddy was the most frequent unexpected caller and she certainly didn't feel like seeing him now. She got out of the bath and wrapped herself in a towel as Francis went to open the door.

'I want to speak to Claire Potter,' she heard a shrill, unknown woman's voice say. Perhaps it was somebody to do with work, someone from a problem family, but how on earth could anyone like that have found out her address?

Through the bathroom door she could hear Francis mumbling something or other, and then she heard the woman's voice again.

'It's a personal matter. I absolutely have to see her.'

She heard the front door slam and then she heard more voices and footsteps so she realised that Francis must have taken the woman into the sitting room.

She had her towel round her but her clothes were in the bedroom which was beyond the sitting room, so she had no means of getting them without confronting this strange woman in her present state of undress. Why the hell hadn't Francis thought of that? He could have taken whoever it was into the kitchen instead. She wondered what to do. She could just wait and hope that it would eventually dawn on Francis that she was somehow trapped in the bathroom. Anyway who was this person and what on earth did they want?

She sat on the side of the bath and looked at her feet. She could still see the white mark left by her shoes in the summer. She stretched out one leg – even her legs had a lingering hint of brown. She had quite nice legs and feet – but why wouldn't that woman go away? Or at least why didn't Francis come to the rescue? She stood up and looked in the mirror, licked her finger and smoothed one eyebrow and then the other. This was deathly boring. She opened the medicine cupboard and looked idly inside. There was a bottle of red nail varnish on the shelf. Perhaps she would paint her toenails. By the time she had done that Francis might have thought of bringing her some clothes or something. She had painted the toenails on one foot and had just started on her second big toe when the bathroom door opened so suddenly that she jumped out of her skin, smudging the nail varnish all over her toe.

Francis stood in the doorway.

'For God's sake come,' he said. 'There's this woman waiting to see you.'

'Shut the door!' said Claire frantically. But she was too late. The woman had followed Francis into the passage and was standing behind him in the bathroom doorway, rudely peering over his shoulder.

'Ah yes, you're Claire Potter,' said the woman. 'I have to speak to you at once.'

Claire was quite overcome with embarrassment and annoyance but somehow she managed to push her way past the two of them as they stood in the doorway, and make a dash for the bedroom.

A few moments later, emerging into the sitting room fully dressed in the clothes she had just taken off, she felt more in control of the situation.

She looked steadily at the woman and took in at a glance the extravagantly dyed red hair, the beaky nose, heavy make-up, huge bosom and blood-red finger nails. She thought of her own smudged toenail and said,

'What is it I can do to help you?'

'I have come to look for my jewels,' said the woman angrily.

Claire had no idea what was going on. She knew nothing about any jewels. It might be better if they sat down.

'Perhaps you could explain yourself,' said Claire. 'What is your name? And what is all this to do with me?'

'I am a friend of Roddy's,' said the red-head. 'Or was.'

Light began to dawn.

'But just you wait until I get my hands on the bastard. I'll ring his neck.'

Claire hastily explained that she had not seen Roddy for some time and that she had no idea where he was.

The woman, who was still standing firmly in the middle of the room, announced that she was called Danny. She'd been seeing Roddy for a few months until a couple of weeks back when he'd been round at her place – in Orchard Close. They'd had ever such a pleasant evening and then they'd gone to bed. Danny had woken up at around two o'clock in the morning to find that Roddy had gone.

'Just walked out on me,' Danny waved a painted hand. Not that she would miss Roddy – oh no, she wasn't bothered about him, there were plenty more fish like him in the sea – and better ones too. So she'd turned over and gone back to sleep. It wasn't until the morning when she was getting dressed that she'd noticed that her rings had gone. A diamond one and an aquamarine. Well everyone knew that Roddy was always short of money but she hadn't expected him to sink to that. Just nicked her rings, he had, and walked out. She might not be bothered about Roddy, but the rings were a different matter. She very much wanted to see them again.

Claire couldn't believe it. There must be some mistake. Of course Roddy would never do a thing like that. He'd probably been called away, on business or something, and he would be bound to get in touch again as soon as he came back.

'Business, my foot!' said Danny.

It did sound pretty feeble, but what on earth else could Claire say? She looked helplessly at Francis who was standing limply by the door, smoking a cigarette.

'I really can't help you,' Claire went on. 'As I say, I haven't seen Roddy and I am sure he can't have taken your rings.'

'Don't you be so sure,' said Danny. 'I wouldn't trust the bastard as far as I could spit. Now, quite frankly would you?' She looked straight at Claire who found herself blushing and avoiding Danny's gaze.

'I went to the police,' Danny went on, 'immediately – but they can't find him. I doubt they took the trouble to look, but I've just about been waiting long enough now. I went round to the police station again today and a young whippersnapper had the nerve to tell me that they'd got nothing to go on, so they've dropped the case. Dropped the bloody case! "And what about my rings?" I said to him. "I suggest you put in an insurance claim Madam," that's what he said to me. Put in an insurance claim and let the bastard off scot free. You just wait till I get hold of him?'

'So why don't you put in an insurance claim?' Francis asked. His back was turned and he was vaguely fiddling with the television aerial.

'Never mind the insurance claim, I want my rings back and I want to find Roddy.' Danny was standing with her shoulders back, her huge breasts thrust forward and one hand on her hip.

Claire had no idea what to do. She just wished the wretched woman would go away. The whole thing was both embarrassing and humiliating.

[125]

'I'm afraid that we have to go out now,' she said. 'If Roddy gets in touch, I'll certainly tell him that you've been looking for him.'

It took quite a long time to get rid of Danny although Claire was never really quite clear as to what Danny hoped to gain by staying. And it occurred to her to wonder how Danny had known where to find her in the first place. It seemed unlikely enough that Roddy would ever have bothered to mention that he had a sister, let alone where she lived. Well, Danny and Roddy had had a rendezvous one evening at the pub down the road and he'd happened to say that he'd just been calling on his sister. Danny always remembered useful things like that about people. You never knew when that sort of information would come in handy.

Eventually Danny left, swearing that she'd be back again to look for Roddy and threatening to go round and call on his parents although Claire begged her not to.

A fat lot Danny cared about his parents' feelings. Roddy should've thought about them before he started going around nicking other people's things.

At last as the door was closed behind Danny, Claire looked at her watch and sighed. They were going to be terribly late for supper and what with one thing and another Claire had rather lost her enthusiasm for the evening.

'I don't think we should have any more to do with Roddy,' said Francis as he followed Claire back into the bedroom where she was going to change. She no longer really cared what she put on.

'It's difficult not to have anything more to do with my brother,' – there was an edge of irritation in her voice – 'whatever he does.'

'He's just a crook,' said Francis, 'and a bloody selfish one. When did he ever do anything for anyone else? And you go on at me, but what's to stop him getting a job?'

'I don't know,' said Claire and sighed, on the verge of tears. She was always crying, or nearly crying these days. What on earth was the matter with her?

'And what a nasty woman. We don't want to get people like her coming round here,' said Francis.

'She wasn't very nice, but let's just not talk or think about Roddy and his problems for a while,' Claire said with a faint smile. 'Come on, let's go,' and she picked up her bag and made for the door.

In the car on the way out to supper, Claire sat at the wheel frowning and worrying about Roddy and her parents. She wondered where the hell he had got to.

Francis wished Claire would stop thinking about Roddy. Roddy might not be his brother, but if he were, Francis wouldn't give him a second thought. He wasn't worth it. If Claire allowed herself to get so worked up about all these people she worked with and about her good-for-nothing brother as well, no wonder she had no time left for him. And she may not have noticed it, but he was at a pretty low ebb at the moment what with one thing and another. He hadn't the faintest idea what he was going to do now the soap opera thing had fallen through.

It was a bloody shame about that. Somehow he'd have to think of something else to write about. He did rather like the idea of writing – but how the hell was he going to find a subject?

He glanced at Claire. Her face was still set in a frown of concentration as she wove through the traffic. Why wouldn't she talk to him? And what was the point of that bloody stupid woman coming around to annoy them? It was all her fault. Hers and Roddy's. Francis wanted Claire to himself. That was why they had had such a good time in Italy – because Claire hadn't had to worry about all those other awful people. She had had time for him for once. He was beginning to feel rather angry and suddenly slightly panicky about his future, and as the anger and the panic grew inside him, he felt an attack of asthma coming on and began to feel desperately in his pocket for his ventilator.

Bugger. He'd left it behind.

'My ventilator,' he began to splutter, and he tapped Claire on the arm. He began to gasp for breath. ' . . .At home . . .' he managed to get out, as he pointed frantically back over his shoulder.

There was nothing for it but to turn round and go back and fetch the damn thing. Without saying anything, and biting back her irritation as she did so, Claire swung round in a dangerous U-turn and was hooted at from all sides. They really were going to be horribly late.

When Francis and Claire eventually arrived at their friends' flat, flustered and aggravated by their own lateness, they were surprised to find a fairly large party in full swing.

Chris and Penny had been together for a couple of years. He was in his last year as a medical student and she had trained as a social worker with Claire. Penny and Chris and Claire and Francis used to see a lot of each other but they had been seeing less of each other lately, mainly because Chris had been working so hard.

'I'm sorry we're so late,' said Claire as she kissed Penny, and then as she kissed Chris, 'We didn't realise it was going to be such a big party.'

'Have some vino,' said Chris. 'Red or white? And help yourself to some food – it's all over there.' He pointed to a table at the end of the room.

'Hi Francis,' he added and gave Francis a friendly great pat on the shoulder with his massive hand. 'How's things? Haven't seen you for ages. What've you been up to?'

Francis shuffled awkwardly and lit a cigarette. He hated people asking him what he'd been up to.

'Oh this and that,' he said, 'not much really.' He thought of saying that he was thinking of writing a book but decided against it. Chris and Penny had been around a lot when he was talking about bridges and he didn't want to bring that up just now.

'We went to Italy,' he said, 'in the summer. Florence and . . .'

'Hi Mike,' Chris interrupted as he spotted another late arrival. 'What'll you have, red or white?'

Francis moved away and followed Claire to the side table

[128]

where the food was laid out. Quite a spread. Someone had been working hard.

Half an hour later Claire was feeling much more relaxed. She had had masses of delicious food and like everybody else she seemed a little drunk. She was sitting on the floor talking to a friend of Chris's – another medical student – and out of the corner of her eye she had noticed Francis sitting on a sofa at the far end of the room talking to a thin girl with long hair.

There were dirty plates everywhere, most of them with cigarettes stubbed out in them and although the window was open, the air was stuffy with smoke. Neither Penny nor Chris smoked, so it must have been pretty nasty for them, but they both looked as if they were enjoying themselves tremendously.

'Penny's looking wonderful, don't you think?' said Claire as Penny topped up her glass.

'Penny's a great girl,' said the medical student with a wink as he held out his glass to be refilled.

Suddenly there was a bellow from the corner of the room and all heads were turned towards Chris who stood there with what looked like a bottle of champagne in his hand.

There was another bellow before silence fell and Chris could make himself properly heard.

'You may all wonder what the hell you're doing here tonight,' he said and there was a drunken titter from the room.

'Well, I'll tell you. Come here, Penny,' he looked around the room with mock anxiety. 'Where are you Penny?'

Penny picked her way through the crowd and stood laughing beside Chris. Chris took her hand and held it up in the air.

'Now this is Penny,' he said. 'You all know Penny, don't you . . .?'

'Not as well as you do,' came a drunken voice from the crowd.

'Now then, keep it clean,' said Chris, and everybody laughed. Penny was laughing too.

'Well Penny's decided at last,' Chris went on bellowing, 'that the time has come for her to make an honest man of me . . . she's asked me to marry her . . .'

There was a roar of laughter from the floor and a great deal of drunken cheering which drowned what Chris was trying to say. He waved his hand in the air for silence and eventually was heard again. Next to him Penny was pink in the face, her eyes sparkling as she grinned adoringly up at the giant beside her.

'She's probably getting a bit broody,' Chris announced. 'You know, thinking of making babies . . .' There was another roar of inane laughter.

'Anyway she seems to think that I look like the right sort of bloke to sire them . . .'

'What've you got that we haven't got?' came another voice from the floor.

'Do you want me to show you?' More ribald laughter as Chris raised one eyebrow in mock query. Penny at his side was growing pinker and pinker by the minute, opening her eyes wide and pretending to ask him to stop.

Claire, sitting in the middle of the laughing crowd, suddenly felt dreadfully alone. Everyone around her seemed so carefree and so happy for Chris and Penny while she felt quite at odds with their mood. She stared hard at the floor hoping that no one would notice her long face. The vulgar jokes and the general merriment were jarring on her nerves as she couldn't help but think of her own future. Would she now ever marry Francis? She could no longer imagine doing so with any delight and yet neither could she imagine leaving him. What would poor Francis do without her? She couldn't possibly envisage him alone. They had been together for five years and it really was, to all intents and purposes, as though they were married – but of course they weren't – and one day she too wanted to have babies. She mustn't leave it too late.

Chris was opening a bottle of Spanish champagne and corks seemed to be flying all over the room. Claire looked up and saw Francis out of the corner of her eye, laughing and joking with the rest of them. She wondered what he was really thinking. How did he see the future? He must sometimes think about it.

Somebody poured some sparkling wine into Claire's glass and she smiled faintly. Then everyone was kissing Penny and patting Chris on the back and shaking his hand and shouting.

Claire made her way through the throng towards Penny. She embraced her warmly but there was a lump in her throat as she said,

'What wonderful news, Penny, I'm so happy for you – when's it to be?'

Then as she kissed Chris he said, 'So what about it Claire? You and Francis – high time you made up your minds isn't it? When are you two going to take the plunge?'

Claire felt like crying again.

'Oh, I don't suppose we ever will,' she said feebly.

Luckily someone else came up to talk to Chris at that moment and she was able to make her getaway and move across the room to where Francis was talking to a different thin girl with short hair.

'I think we ought to be going,' she said, looking at her watch. 'It's getting quite late and I've got to be at work early in the morning.'

Francis didn't really want to go. He was enjoying himself and hadn't been to such a good party for a long time. But after a few minutes he allowed himself to be dragged reluctantly away.

As they said good-bye Chris playfully punched Francis and said,

'I say, old man, what about it? Your turn next. I've already had a word with Claire,' and he caught hold of her arm and pulled her towards him to prevent her from leaving. 'You can't keep us all in suspense any longer or we'll begin to think you're never going to pop the question.'

Francis laughed weakly and put his arm round Claire.

'Oh, we're not in any hurry,' he said. 'Anyway we're happy as we are, aren't we?' He turned to look at Claire and smiled inanely.

'Well, come on,' said Claire brusquely. 'We must be going. Thanks for a lovely party!' And she almost ran for the door, dragging Francis behind her.

'Jolly good party,' Francis said when they were in the car. 'Did you enjoy it?'

'Not really,' said Claire, and large tears started suddenly to roll down her cheeks. She sniffed and wiped her nose with the back of her hand. The car swerved dangerously.

'For God's sake be careful,' said Francis, and then realising that she was crying, asked in amazement, 'What on earth's the matter?'

'Everything,' said Claire, 'absolutely everything.'

Francis thought that Claire must have had too much to drink – not that she was in the habit of drinking too much, but then neither was she in the habit of bursting into tears when she left a party. He simply couldn't think what to say and they drove on home in silence apart from an occasional sniff from Claire.

When they reached the flat Claire decided to make some tea.

Francis would have been perfectly happy to stay on at the party but now that he was home, he really felt like going to bed. But as Claire was obviously rather upset he thought that perhaps he ought to have a cup of tea with her. Perhaps she would tell him what was troubling her. God only knew.

'Doesn't it ever occur to you that it's rather depressing us just going on like this?' said Claire tearfully, as she sipped her tea. 'There's you without a job – without any life plan,' she sniffed, 'and us, well, not really knowing what's going to happen . . .'

'What do you mean, not knowing what's going to happen? We've always known what's going to happen. We're just waiting to see . . .'

'To see what, for Christ's sake?' Claire almost yelled.

'To see what's going to happen, of course.'

[132]

'Francis, you're mad. Can't you ever look at anything from anyone else's point of view but your own?' She picked up her empty mug, carried it to the sink and, taking a handkerchief out of her pocket, blew her nose. 'I'm always trying to see things how you see them, but do you ever even bother to suppose that I may see them differently myself?'

Claire wasn't making any sense at all. She was obviously in a state and there was no point in discussing things with her in that frame of mind. There was no doubt about it, she must have had a bit too much to drink at the party.

'Let's go to bed,' said Francis, 'you'll feel better in the morning. We can discuss everything then.'

Francis of course would be asleep in the morning.

'If we leave it much longer, there'll be nothing left to discuss,' said Claire ominously and went into the bathroom and slammed the door. She was feeling very emotional. Perhaps she had had a little too much to drink after all.

CHAPTER XII

When Roddy was fifteen a dreadful thing happened. A fourteen-year-old girl in his class at school became pregnant. She said that Roddy was responsible and subsequently had an abortion.

Roddy, of course, claimed that the girl had done the same thing with all the boys in the class and that she was just a slag. But she, backed up by her furious parents, denied it, saying that Roddy was the only one. When confronted by this evidence, Roddy merely gave a cavalier shrug and said that it was obvious that she would lie – wasn't it?

It was put to him that to some people it might also seem obvious that he would lie.

'Lie? What? Me?' he said, jabbing at his chest with his forefinger and looking innocently around. Why should he lie? Of course he might be the father but then as there were eleven other boys in the class, he only had a one in twelve chance.

George was furious. What did the boy mean by talking in that glib fashion? He deserved a damn good hiding. None of this would have happened if Roddy had been sent away to a good, old-fashioned boarding school.

Even Nancy who, abreast of the times, had always been one hundred percent in favour of co-education, was wondering if it wasn't a mistake after all. Perhaps temptation should not be put in the way of teenagers who were too young to cope emotionally or too immature to be responsible for their actions. But when she looked around at her friends' children, most of them seemed to be able to cope all right. They were, on the whole, nice, polite, bright, well-balanced children, and in her heart of hearts she knew that it was Roddy who was at fault and not the system. If he had gone to a single-sex boarding school, he would have found some other way of getting into trouble. She could feel it in her bones and if she allowed herself to dwell on it, her blood ran cold with fear for the future.

And, worst of all, she must be partly to blame, for she, Roddy's own mother, had shown so little faith in him. She could not forget hurling him angrily into the desecrated bed of tulips and neither could she forget her words at the time – spiteful . . . evil . . . hateful . . . a disappointment from the word go.

Nancy felt that she must talk to the boy and see if she could somehow get through to him – not to make him guilty, oh no, but just to make him realise that he should have some sense of responsibility. She was not against the sexual revolution which had taken place – on the contrary, if only it had happened earlier she might not have been burdened for all these years with a sense of guilt about Gregory; but fourteen and fifteen year olds were a bit on the young side, and even Nancy was not so naive as to suppose that Roddy had been involved in anything like what was nowadays called 'a meaningful relationship'.

Where George was morally and emotionally one hundred percent against abortion on any grounds whatsoever, Nancy had a rather different outlook. She believed that women had a right to make their own decisions about such matters and that in certain cases abortion might be definitely advisable, but when she contemplated the trauma which this child must have suffered and which might leave her scarred forever, she was disgusted and ashamed of having in any way been connected with the matter.

Both she and George with their different attitudes were appalled, saddened and disappointed by the whole affair, and in Nancy's opinion, there was no point in punishing Roddy – in any case how could he be punished? She must take it upon herself to talk to him.

So one day when they were alone in the kitchen, Nancy tried to talk to Roddy and to point out to him how, as a result of his, and indeed her own, irresponsible attitude, the girl had been made to suffer.

Roddy didn't seem to take in what she was saying at all.

'You know nothing about it,' he said rudely. 'Sex wasn't even invented in your day I gather. Young people are different now. As far as she's concerned it's just lucky they've made abortion legal. It can't have hurt her. She only missed one day at school. Teach her to be more careful next time,' he added with a supercilious snigger.

Nancy thought of the poor girl lying white-faced in a hospital bed and of all the ghastly humiliation involved in the whole filthy business and she felt her stomach heave.

'You understand nothing,' she said, looking straight at Roddy. 'Nothing.'

He looked back and his gaze faltered for a moment as he met her eyes and then, in a flash, he was smiling, his charming, disarming smile.

'Come on, Mum,' he said in a conciliatory tone, 'there's no need to make such a fuss about nothing. I reckon you're just jealous of all the sex we're getting.' Then he added with a hint of provocation in his voice, and with one eyebrow raised, 'Feeling you missed out a bit perhaps?'

For the second time in her life, Nancy lost her temper with Roddy. She slapped him as hard as she could across the face.

'I say, cool it,' said Roddy. 'There's no need to get violent,' and with one arm he pushed his mother aside and strode nonchalantly out of the room, leaving Nancy to collapse in tears, her head buried in her arms on the kitchen table.

Later Nancy apologised to Roddy for having hit him. He accepted her apology graciously but still couldn't think why she had got so worked up.

'The trouble with you, Mum,' he said kindly, 'is that you're just out of tune with the times. And, another thing – you go on all the time about guilt and never wanting to make us feel guilty and all that and then you stand there trying to instil guilt into us. I don't get it.'

Nancy didn't get it either. She quietly left the room.

In the months which followed, Nancy grew increasingly anxious about Roddy. She sometimes even went so far as to wonder if he were really a very nice person. George was a nice person and Claire was a nice person – she could be tiresome at times, but she was definitely a nice person – and she, Nancy, was quite a nice person – well, she didn't honestly think that other people were very likely to describe her as a nasty person, but Roddy was different. She felt that she had really to concentrate on Roddy's nicer sides in order to persuade herself that he was a nice person. He had a lovely smile and could be very affectionate at times – but then sometimes she even felt that he was only affectionate when he wanted something. No. That was unfair. Of course it was unfair. And then, he was nice to animals. She thought he was always nice to animals. Nancy had forgotten how Roddy used to leave the cage door open for Claire's hamster to escape, and how he used to tread on the kitten's tail.

The problem of guilt and conscience exercised Nancy considerably at this time and occasionally she broached the subject with George, but George as usual was so cut and dried in his opinions that there was little room for conversation. He couldn't really see what all the fuss was about as if you felt guilty it probably meant that you had done wrong and if you had done wrong it was only right that you should feel guilty.

For Nancy there were some things which she had been taught to believe were wrong but which she herself didn't really feel were wrong. George told her that she wouldn't be troubled by such worries if she adhered strictly to a religion, but she wasn't sure that he was right. No religion could provide all the answers. People who thought they

[137]

knew best, said George, were indulging in the sin of pride. But as far as Nancy could see George was merely lacking in imagination and understanding.

Then there was social guilt which George didn't seem to understand at all, although he felt genuinely sorry for the victims of natural disasters and for the sick so that he regularly and without any fuss gave a proportion of his salary to charity. But he saw no reason to dwell on the plight of others or to torture himself about it unnecessarily. Do your best, he would say, by your own code and there will be no room for guilt.

But Nancy wasn't satisfied. She suggested that George did feel social guilt and that it was only that which made him give regularly to charity.

If that was the case, guilt must have a positive side since the charities concerned could well do with the money, George replied, and turned his mind back to the crossword.

Nancy herself definitely had a social conscience. For years now – since both the children had been at full time school – she had given a great deal of her time and energy to raising money for cancer relief, for kidney machines, for Oxfam and for the Spastics Society. She knew quite well that the work she did was of as much benefit to herself as to the organisations she worked for and sometimes she felt guilty about that.

George thought she was being silly. She was doing a useful job for which other people were grateful and all she had to do was to stop making a fuss and to get on with it.

Of course she knew that in this case George was right and that if she carried her own train of thought too far she would end up feeling guilty for even existing which would be quite ridiculous. It was funny how the problem of guilt had dogged her all her life. Well it certainly didn't look as if it was going to dog Roddy. That in itself must be a good thing, provided that he could at least be taught to discover the difference between right and wrong.

'Your idea of what is right may well not be the same as mine, Mother dear,' Roddy said to her rudely one day.

'It doesn't look as though it is,' she answered sadly. She didn't know how to go on from there and picked up a newspaper and disappeared behind it.

'Just learn to consider other people,' she said without looking up a few moments later. But there was no answer as Roddy had crept out of the room and out of the house and was off to meet some cronies.

Roddy was always on Nancy's mind. Whenever the telephone rang she would run to answer it, anxious that a schoolmaster or an angry parent might be ringing to complain about his behaviour. She wondered what on earth he would do next and her mood swung between fearful pessimism and buoyant optimism. What on earth would happen to him as he grew older? How would this lazy, bright, callous boy cope with the adult world?

But then she shouldn't worry so. He would eventually grow up and learn to shoulder his responsibilities like a man. After all, she shouldn't expect too much from him when he was so young – and fifteen was a notoriously difficult age.

One day, just before lunch, her mind racing as usual along these lines, Nancy was on her way back from a fund-raising meeting when she decided to pop into the bank to pay in a few cheques which had been sent to Cancer Relief.

There seemed to be three or four people waiting for every cashier. Nancy joined what looked like the fastest moving queue, but soon realised that she had made a mistake as there was a woman who seemed to be paying in the whole of Woolworth's takings for a week. She looked at her watch. Oh well, she wasn't really in that much of a hurry. She shifted her weight from one foot to the other and began to wonder what she was going to give the family for supper.

Eventually the woman who had been paying in so much money gathered up her things and moved away, and a man, two in front of Nancy, moved up to take her place.

Nancy hadn't noticed him until then and now, as she stared at his back, she just wished he would hurry up. Then she heard his voice.

[139]

Her heart missed a beat and then began to pound furiously. She felt electrified by that old, half-forgotten feeling of intense excitement. She dared not move but in a minute he would turn round and when he did he might not see her and if he did he might not recognise her. What if he didn't recognise her? Could she have changed so much? Her legs felt weak. She patted her hair nervously, hoping that it didn't look too much of a mess. Eternity seemed to be captured in that minute.

Then he turned round, stuffing his wallet into his inside pocket as he did so, and started towards the door of the bank when suddenly he saw her. An expression of utter delight lit up his face.

'It's Nancy!' he said. 'After all these years! Nancy! And you haven't changed at all!'

Nancy, oblivious of everything and everyone else, dropped her bag to the floor, and flung her arms round his neck.

'Gregory!' she said. 'How wonderful to see you!'

Gregory, Nancy thought as she gazed at him later, had grown better looking with age – it was eighteen years since they had last seen each other. He had a confident and relaxed manner and seemed quite unlike the shy, rather awkward young man she remembered, although he had the same kind face and frank gaze – and of course the same, unforgettable voice.

They were sitting in a pub having a drink for old times' sake and a bite of lunch. Nancy hardly ever went to pubs and never drank in the middle of the day and she vaguely wondered what people she knew would think if they saw her. Not that it mattered a pin what they thought. This was a special occasion.

Gregory told her that he still worked in insurance but was now with a firm in central London. He had just come out to this neck of the woods to see a client and had to get back to his office after lunch. He lived in Fulham now, and had done for some years. But what about Nancy?

She told him all about her life since they had last met – he had heard years ago that she was married – she told him about George and about her children and her charity work and she told him that her grandmother had died but that her mother was still alive although rather old and doddering now. There was nothing else which she could think of which might interest him and anyway she was dying to hear more about Gregory. Was he married?

Yes he was married although he hadn't been married as long as Nancy. His agoraphobic mother – poor thing – had grown gradually sicker and sicker so that life at home in those days had been pretty difficult and he had sometimes thought that he would go mad himself.

'I missed you a lot, Nancy, you know and felt very badly about you,' he said, and dared to touch her hand. 'So many times I nearly rang you. But I never did you see. I'm sorry . . .'

'Well, it's too late now,' said Nancy, and laughed.

In the end his mother had got so bad that she had to go to hospital. There was no alternative.

'She only died last year,' he said.

After she went into hospital Gregory's life changed drastically, of course, and things became much easier for him although he had felt pretty guilty about his mother for a long time, but there was nothing else he could have done as she was apparently incurable and there had come a point when he couldn't even leave her alone for a night. He moved out of the house, found a flat and changed jobs and then, a few years later, he'd married.

He had been married for nearly twelve years now – to an Australian nurse. In fact Lesley was in Australia at the moment. She had gone back to see her mother because her father had just died. She'd be away for a month. It was so expensive to get there that it hardly seemed worthwhile to go for a shorter time.

Lesley and Gregory had ten-year-old twin sons who were away at boarding school. That had been Lesley's idea. She was very impressed by old-fashioned English education and she thought that boarding school would make gentlemen of her little boys. Gregory laughed. He wasn't so sure about that. Anyway what with the boys being away and Lesley being in Australia, Gregory was pretty much on his own at the moment. At a bit of a loose end and as free as air.

Nancy looked straight into his eyes. Was he making a proposition? She supposed so but then she could hardly claim to be as free as air herself. In fact she couldn't remember any period of her life when she had been.

'Well,' she suddenly said, looking at her watch, 'I think I ought to be getting on. But it's been lovely to see you again, Gregory. It really has.' She looked at him and smiled.

It was time for Gregory to be heading back to his office, too.

'Can I give you a lift?' he asked, as they left the pub.

'Oh, no thank you,' said Nancy. 'It's only a few minutes walk.'

But Gregory insisted that they should meet again. Couldn't Nancy come in to London one day and he'd give her lunch – not in a pub – but in a proper restaurant?

Nancy was delighted by the idea. Certainly she was free enough for that and of course she would come – so they made a date for two days later.

It was late June and there had recently been a general election at which Edward Heath had won an unexpected victory and George and many others at the time were fascinated by the new government and could talk of nothing else. That evening George was glued to the television again and not particularly interested in anything Nancy had to say. She didn't really mind. After all, if it wasn't the General Election it was the crossword – or Dvořák. George was never a particularly chatty sort. In any case she had no intention of telling him about Gregory. He knew that she had had a walk out with Gregory years ago, but the two had never met and Nancy had never discussed Gregory with George nor ever intended to.

For the next two days Nancy could think of nothing but Gregory. She daydreamed about him ceaselessly and wondered what she would wear for the lunch, where he would take her and how their renewed relationship would

[142]

develop – if develop it did. She sang about her daily chores, fantasised about love in the afternoon, longed for intrigue, yearned for Gregory's arms about her and for a blissful interlude forgot her troubles, her guilt and her quite impossible son.

At lunch, when they met in a small Italian restaurant, Gregory told her that he had taken the afternoon off, and so after lunch all her dreams came true.

Nancy's new affair with Gregory lasted for a little over a year. In the first few weeks it was made easier by Lesley's absence in Australia but even then it was not always easy for Nancy to get away from home. When Lesley came home, rendezvous were even more difficult to arrange. Gregory could hardly take every afternoon off and weekends were out of the question. Sometimes they met for lunch, but in fact had no time for lunch and at other times they met in the early evening when Nancy would pretend that she had been at a fund-raising meeting. Occasionally Nancy would say that she had to go and visit her mother, but she was terrified of being caught out in these lies.

In fact, George seemed quite unsuspicious and never asked any awkward questions, which at least made things a little easier.

Thirteen-year-old Claire remarked, once or twice, that her mother seemed particularly busy at the time, and then, and only then, Nancy felt a pang of remorse.

As for Roddy – his mother's more frequent absences from home in the evenings made it easier for him to go about his own nefarious business and he certainly didn't miss her.

Sometimes Nancy was amazed by her own behaviour and even more amazed by her lack of burning guilt; what guilt she did feel, she seemed, for once in her life, to be enjoying. Existence had taken on a new dimension. She felt excited and pretty and carefree as the days between her meetings with Gregory passed in a dreamy haze. The days with him were unlike any other days in her life, alive and thrilling, so that all the intrigue and all the lies seemed worth it.

[143]

After ten months of intrigue and glorious sex such as Nancy had never known with George, Gregory suggested that he should leave Lesley and she should leave George. They had already wasted eighteen years and they should waste no more.

Nancy was horrified. She knew that marriage to Gregory would not be the same as this joyful affair. She loathed the idea of breaking up her home, of making her children miserable and of breaking poor George's innocent heart. She loved Gregory in a way, but even more she loved the spice which her affair with him added to her life. Besides it gave her a feeling of independence, of being in control of things and of having her own identity – but she definitely did not want the responsibility of two broken marriages on her hands.

Gregory could not take 'no' for an answer. He pestered and pestered and began to pity himself. He would never have married Lesley in the first place if he could have married Nancy. Lesley was bossy and cold and didn't understand him. She didn't like sex very much, she was a bad mother, a bad cook and, for all he knew, a bad nurse.

Nancy pointed out that perhaps he was a bad husband. He was certainly a disloyal one and then they had their first big row. They were lying in bed in a hotel in Earl's Court at three o'clock in the afternoon and as they quarrelled it seemed to Nancy that all the innocence and joy in their relationship had disappeared to be replaced by tawdry, everyday squalor, cheap betrayal and cliché.

She got out of bed and dressed with tears streaming down her face and left for home. The same argument occurred next time they met and then they began to meet less and less often. Nancy began to make excuses. It was easy enough for her to make an excuse for not being able to get away.

At last the day came for them to say good-bye and it was to Nancy as though she had exorcised her youth. From her own point of view she couldn't help feeling that she had got away unharmed after what had been a glorious interlude, an escapist dream which ceased to enchant her as soon as it became tainted with reality. But she did feel sorry for Gregory and, once again, guilty. As far as she could see, there was no experience in life which left you free from guilt. She of all people should have realised that most of all a love affair was bound to cause it somewhere along the line, particularly in a person like herself, and she turned her concentration back to her everyday life, there was guilt everywhere.

How she had abandoned her son, ignored her daughter, not loved her husband sufficiently, forgotten her flower garden, skipped charity meetings, thought only of herself and even – perhaps – broken Gregory's heart. She tried to tell herself that the whole thing was just as much Gregory's fault as hers, that none of her family had been irrevocably hurt, that it had only been a brief and at times ecstatically happy interlude, and that the flower garden could soon be put to rights again, but whichever way she looked at it, she could never rid herself of her old demon and once again she blamed her upbringing. Surely her children would never feel haunted by such useless guilt.

CHAPTER XIII

Francis remembered, as he lay in bed one morning, that years ago when he was a child he had been watching a television programme called 'Blue Peter' on which there was a man who had made an amazing model of the Taj Mahal using twenty-five thousand, two hundred and forty-eight matchsticks. Or thirty-six thousand, seven hundred and thirty-six. Anyway something like that. He must have been a pretty clever sort of fellow. Francis began to wonder how many matches had in fact been involved and how big the model had been.

Making a model like that could be quite fun – and demanding too, no doubt. You'd need a hell of a lot of bloody patience, though. One thing about Francis was that he was quite patient – no one could deny it, but he'd never have the patience to do a thing like that. Of course you'd also have to be quite good with your hands. Francis wondered whether the man on 'Blue Peter' had painted the model of the Taj Mahal and whether the model itself had been shown on the television. Of course it must have been but, for some reason, Francis couldn't remember it. And neither, for that matter, could he remember if the man had made any other models besides the one of the Taj Mahal. He supposed he had because he'd have had to be a bloody genius to start on the Taj Mahal without having made anything else first.

Francis wasn't sure exactly what the Taj Mahal looked like although he must have seen pictures of it, but he thought it had a lot of minarets and domes and things. How on earth had that fellow made those domes and minarets with matchsticks? Perhaps if you soaked a matchstick in water it would bend like wire. Francis wondered. Anyone wanting to make those sorts of models would be well advised to start on something a bit more straightforward than the Taj Mahal anyway – something more like Buckingham Palace.

It was probably time Francis began to think about getting out of bed. He looked at his watch. Ten thirty. Well, he'd give himself a few more minutes and then he'd go down and buy some fags and think what to do next. He sniffed. It was a bloody nuisance about his cold – he thought he'd got rid of it at last but it seemed to be coming back. Perhaps he'd caught another one off himself.

He lay back in bed and went on thinking about the Taj Mahal and trying to work out how the hell that man had made minarets and cupolas out of matchsticks.

Later on he went down to the supermarket for his cigarettes and to do a bit of shopping which he'd promised he'd do for Claire. There were several things on her list, including matches – they were always running out of them. He stared at the shelves piled high with matchboxes wondering which ones to buy. Swan Vestas were good, but the boxes were too big to put in your pocket – or he could buy one of those big packs of six or eight boxes but the trouble with them was that anyone who came to the flat seemed to pocket a box and the whole lot disappeared overnight. Perhaps he'd buy one of those very big boxes of Ship safety matches to leave by the stove in the kitchen and one small box for his own pocket.

Why was it that everything in life seemed so complicated – even down to buying matches. He picked up a big box of safety matches and studied the front of it. He was surprised to see that the matches were made in Sweden. Not that he'd ever really thought about where they were made before, and they had to be made somewhere, so why not Sweden? He quite liked the picture of the sailing ship on the front and wondered what it was – a clipper or a schooner? He didn't know which but either way it was quite nice really. Still it must have been pretty good hell going to sea in those days – everybody vomiting all over the place and rats for companions as well. There was an average of three hundred matches in the box – or so it said. That was quite surprising. Francis would have thought that there would have been something more like five hundred.

That man who made the model of the Taj Mahal must have had to buy a hell of a lot of bloody matches. Supposing the model had even taken as many as twenty thousand matches, he would have had to buy . . . Francis tried to divide twenty-thousand by three hundred in his head. He used to be quite good at mental arithmetic but he was rather out of practice. He knocked off a few noughts and did the sum over again just to check. Sixty-six point six recurring. That seemed like a pretty silly sort of number and anyway he would have needed a few more in case some of the matches got broken. Actually sixty-six – never mind the point six recurring – weren't really all that many boxes of matches when you came to think about it.

Francis wondered how much sixty-six boxes of matches would cost. He twisted the box around in his hand looking for the price. Nothing seemed to have a price label on it any more these days – only those silly lines for computers. He glanced at the shelf underneath the matches and saw that they cost 36p a box. He wondered how many boxes he could run to. He was suddenly really attracted to the idea of building something with matches – in fact he thought he'd have a bash at Buckingham Palace. Buckingham Palace ought to be quite easy as it was a plain enough building. It hadn't occurred to him that he didn't know what the garden side of the palace looked like. He'd start with a dozen boxes which would cost less than a fiver and when he'd used them all up, he'd come back for more. All at once he felt filled with a childish enthusiasm and couldn't wait to get home and start work. If he made a good job of it, he would be bound to be able to sell his model, probably for quite a lot of money. He might even be asked to appear on television himself. In these days of mass unemployment people had to show initiative and turn their minds to all sorts of unusual things which no one would ever have considered doing years ago.

Francis paid for his shopping and hurried home, stopping only at the newsagent's shop to buy some glue and a tourist guide to London with a picture of Buckingham Palace in it.

As soon as he reached home, he spread the picture and the matches out on the kitchen table and began to work out the scale of his model. He thought that he would begin with the centre of the façade and build gradually out towards the sides, using the height of two matches as the height of the central ground floor arch. Carefully and meticulously he started to glue matches together, imagining as he did so the perfection of his finished creation, when suddenly it dawned on him that not only had he no idea what the garden façade looked like, but he would need to know about the sides, the Royal stables and even the roof as well before he could do the thing properly. He couldn't think why he hadn't thought about that before. He would have to go back out and find some more pictures of the palace and as he probably wouldn't find anything good enough in the newsagent's, he would have to go all the way to W H Smith. He was sure that they'd have something there in among all those books about royalty.

On his way to W H Smith's he passed the Bricklayers Arms and as it was about half-past one and he hadn't had any lunch yet, he thought he might just as well pop in for a moment and a quick one. He wouldn't stay long as he wanted to get on with his model. He knew that sometimes he just popped into the Bricklayers for a quick one and managed to stay there for a couple of hours. But that was different. If you were out of work and had nothing particular to do, you could hardly be blamed for whiling your time away in the pub. He pushed his way through the swing door, and as he walked over to the bar to order his drink, he noticed quite a few regulars sitting around.

'You seem full of the joys of spring today, Francis,' one of them said. 'What's got into you? Won the pools or something?'

'Oh no,' said Francis, laughing, 'Nothing like that. I've just got a new project on hand.' He didn't want to say what the project was for fear of being laughed at. It did sound a bit silly. He just wouldn't say a word until he'd built the first model. Then they'd all see. Probably see him on television for that matter.

'What is it this time then?' asked one man. 'Bridges, soap operas, jewellery-making – boat-building – breeding goldfish?' He clicked his fingers and looked around at the assembled company to raise a laugh. 'Never mind, son, you're bound to make your fortune in the end if you keep up the good ideas.'

Francis felt silly and slightly piqued but he was so thrilled with his idea that he couldn't be bothered to be cross.

'No,' he said, 'I'd rather not mention it yet. It involves a certain amount of planning.'

'Oh come on Francis, give us a break,' said the man.

Francis at first refused steadfastly to say another word but by the time he had finished his drink and the inquisitive man had offered him the second half he was feeling far more relaxed and less guarded.

But he soon regretted saying anything. What on earth gave those buggers the right to laugh at him? Not one of them had a job of work and none of them did anything all day, as far as he could see, but loaf around down at the betting shop or sit on their backsides boozing. Just because he had a bit of initiative and the occasional bright idea, they thought they could make fun of him.

He downed his drink quickly and walked out of the pub in a sulk to cries of 'Don't take on so, Francis, we were only taking the micky,' and, 'Come on son, can't you take a joke . . .?'

[150]

'Bleeding hell,' said someone as the door swung shut behind him, 'the boy's a bloody nutter.'

Francis walked on down the street towards W H Smith's where he spent a considerable amount of time looking for what he wanted. Eventually he found a book with an aerial view of the Palace and a good picture of it from the garden side. It was a bit of a blow to discover that on the garden side there were rounded steps and a sort of rounded portico thing as well, so he would have to discover how to bend the matches after all.

Or he could just not do Buckingham Palace, but find some other stately home or something which didn't have anything but straight lines. Anyway he bought the book which nearly cleaned him out and began to make his way home.

He had hardly walked a few yards when he heard someone call his name and turned round to see a boy he had worked with as a filing clerk in the solicitor's office.

'How're you then, Paul?' said Francis. 'What are you up to these days?'

'Out of a job,' said Paul, and grinned. 'Same as you?'

'Same as me,' said Francis, 'but . . .' He decided not to go on. He didn't want to risk being laughed at again.

'Doing anything this afternoon?' said Paul.

'Nothing much,' said Francis as he glanced down at the paper bag in his hand. 'No, not really.'

'Let's go for a drink.'

'Yeah, fine,' said Francis, 'I'd love to, but we'd better be quick or it'll be closing time – and let's not go to the Bricklayers Arms. It's a foul pub.'

Paul and Francis stayed in the pub until closing time, then they strolled round to the betting shop where Paul wanted to put some money on a horse. He'd been given a brilliant tip by a friend for the 3.30 at Kempton. It was a certainty – because this friend of Paul's knew one of the lads who worked for the trainer. Out of the horse's mouth you might say.

They hung around the betting shop until after the race

which was a bitter disappointment as Paul's horse came in sixth, and then, wondering what to do to cheer themselves up, they decided to go down to the new amusement arcade which had just been opened in the High Street. They hung around there for a while but had soon both run out of money so they strolled aimlessly away.

Paul looked at his watch, wondering what to do next and suggested that Francis might like to come around to his place to listen to some tapes. Francis thought that sounded like a good idea but by the time he had been at Paul's flat for half an hour he began to get bored. He didn't like Paul's taste in music and there was nothing to drink in the flat, and anyway he had begun to think about Buckingham Palace again, so he made his excuses and returned home.

When he got home he found, to his intense irritation, that he had lost the book he had bought with the aerial view of Buckingham Palace. He wondered what the hell he had done with it. He might have left it at Paul's, but somehow he didn't remember having it when he arrived there which meant that he might have left it by any one of a dozen machines in the amusement arcade, or he might have left it at the betting shop – or in the pub where he and Paul had gone for a drink. He didn't fancy retracing his steps around all those places, and, in any case, it had begun to rain quite hard. He would just have to manage without the picture. He could easily get on with the front façade and find another picture tomorrow. Come to that – the picture in the book had been a pretty rotten one and wouldn't have been much use really.

Claire had been in court all morning giving evidence for a mother who was fighting to prevent her ex-husband from removing her children. When she got back to her office, she felt quite exhausted and worried by all her paperwork which was piling up.

She had just sat down to her desk when the telephone rang. It was the social worker who had been trying to contact Mrs Flack at her mother's house. According to the mother the family had moved back to Thackeray Buildings so perhaps Claire could go round and see them there.

She decided she would go on her way home from work that evening. Meanwhile she would ring the school to see if Yolande was back there.

The schoolteacher reported that in fact Yolande hadn't been seen for some time now which worried Claire who was beginning to be quite concerned that the child might have been badly harmed physically. Time was going by and nobody seemed able to produce any evidence that Yolande was all right.

By the time Claire called at Thackeray Buildings, it was dark and she was longing to get home, but she knew that she mustn't leave the call until the next day.

She banged heavily on the door and waited. There was no sound from inside, not even from the dog, Barry, so she banged again and hardly waited a moment this time before she heard footsteps approaching and the door was immediately opened by Gary.

'Oh it's Claire,' he said. 'Hello darlin', come on in.'

Claire suddenly felt awkward, and hesitated before stepping over the threshold.

'Come on in then,' Gary repeated. 'I just made myself a pot of tea. You can share it with me.'

'I thought that your wife would be back,' said Claire, still strangely embarrassed by Gary's easy familiarity.

'She's still at her mum's,' said Gary. 'I don't know what to do about them poor kids. Did the social worker down there get to see them?'

As they went into the kitchen Claire explained what had happened. Gary wasn't surprised. Alma's mum wouldn't allow anyone to poke their nose into her business. But, as he'd said before, he was sure that the children would come to no real harm while they were with her. He'd been thinking and it seemed to him that Alma and her mum were scared of anyone seeing the marks on Yolande's body.

'When they do come back, I'll have to make sure I see

[153]

them,' said Claire. 'And then there's the problem of school. Yolande should be at school.'

'Well, sit down now and have some tea,' said Gary. 'You look as if you could do with it.'

Claire was surprised, but she sat down.

Gary put the teapot and some mugs on the table.

'I've bin and got myself a job,' he said. 'Started today on a building site. I was just cooking some tea.'

Claire felt that she ought to be going, and leaving Gary to his tea. She had noticed the baked beans in a grubby pan on the oven, some fish fingers frying beside them and two pieces of toasted sliced bread which lay on the table growing cold and hard.

'Why don't you have tea with me?' Gary suggested. 'I've got plenty and it's dull eating alone.'

Claire didn't know why she accepted. Partly out of a mixture of politeness, friendliness and pity, and partly because she liked being there and because she liked Gary. And it was precisely because she did like being there and because she did like Gary that she should have refused and just drunk her mug of tea and gone.

She glanced up nervously at Gary as he put the beans on toast and the fish fingers down in front of her, and caught his eye. He smiled a frank, engaging smile and she smiled back.

Claire thought of Francis. Poor Francis. What was he doing at the moment? she wondered. He was probably sitting smoking in front of the television and waiting for her to come home. She should have been back by now anyway. She munched her baked beans in silence and then accepted a cigarette which Gary offered her. Gary hadn't spoken either. She wondered if he was thinking about his children. She couldn't think of anything to say.

'So what time do you knock off work then?' Gary asked.

'Oh, any time between about five and six. Sometimes I call on people on the way home and that makes me a bit later. Actually I was on my way home when I came here.'

'How long've you been in the job then?'

[154]

Claire began to explain in detail about her years of training, but she broke off suddenly, thinking she was being boring.

'It's nice seeing you,' said Gary. 'It's a bit lonely without the kids and its not the sort of thing I can talk about much with me mates.'

Then they sat chatting for a while about Gary's new job on the building site, about how they liked baked beans, about a programme Gary had seen about AIDS on television the night before and about what a rotten old world it was. Then they talked about the Princess of Wales who had been in the news recently and about how it was all right for some but how they didn't really envy her way of life. Then they talked about football hooligans and government cuts and inflation and unemployment and Mrs Thatcher and poor old Denis and Mark Thatcher who'd done all right for himself and President Reagan who was a clown, and nuclear waste and how Gary didn't want his kids growing up in a world where they might be killed any day by a leak from a nuclear power station if they weren't blown up by American or Russian bombs. It didn't make much difference which. And all the time they were talking, they were drinking tea and smoking. Claire couldn't think what had come over her. She didn't usually smoke more than one cigarette every so often.

She stubbed out a cigarette and looked at her watch.

'Good Lord!' she said, 'I must go. I've been here for hours.'

'Stay as long as you like,' said Gary. 'It's nice seeing you.'

Claire smiled and shook her head and stood up.

'No,' she said, 'I really must go, but let me help you wash up first.'

'Don't be daft,' said Gary.

But Claire picked up her plate and her mug and carried them across to the sink, then, as she turned round Gary was standing just in front of her.

'Thanks for the tea,' she said. 'It was great . . .'

When Gary kissed her she knew that that was what she

had been waiting for all along. In fact she had been waiting for it almost since the first day she saw him in the street before she even knew who he was. He held her tight and he smelt of sweat and frying and cigarettes and she loved him.

'Oh God,' she said as she disentangled herself with tears in her eyes, 'I must go. This is terribly unprofessional.'

'Bugger that,' said Gary and kissed her again.

Then she really did go. She had to. Francis would wonder what on earth had happened to her – she never usually came home so late.

Gary saw her to the door and then said he'd walk down to the car with her. He thought he'd go and find some mates in a pub on the corner.

As they reached the car, Claire thanked him again for the tea. She tilted her head to one side, feeling awkward again.

'It was great,' she said, 'really great,' and she touched him gently on the arm. Then she got into her car and was away.

As she drove home she thought again about Francis. She would just have to tell him that she had been involved in a difficult case and that she had had a lot of paperwork to catch up on – all of which was true. He would have to believe her.

Then she thought of Gary. Gary was wonderful, there was no doubt about that, and there was no doubt either that she was quite in love with him which meant, she knew, that she would have to hand the Flack case over to a colleague but she asked herself what excuse on earth she could find for doing so.

She wondered if she would see Gary again. She knew that she shouldn't. Any further involvement would be bound to bring disaster . . . She could lose everything – Francis, her job, her self-respect – all for a roll in the hay. She imagined the scandal it would cause in her office if she had an affair with Gary. She could see the wounded, puzzled look on the

[156]

face of Barry, her trusting team leader, and a feeling of overwhelming embarrassment suffused her.

The only thing to do was to leave it for a few days and see what happened. It was hardly worth making such a fuss about a kiss. And it was only a kiss.

As Claire opened the door to the flat, feeling all hot and bothered, she heard Francis call from the kitchen.

'There you are at last! What on earth happened to you? I thought you'd had an accident.'

Claire walked into the kitchen and was amazed by what she saw.

'What on earth are you doing?' she asked. 'With all those matches?'

'Bloody matches,' said Francis. 'I had this brilliant idea, but I'm not sure I'm going to be able to do it.'

Claire looked at Francis sitting at the table and suddenly all her old maternal instincts rushed to the fore. He was so pale, so beautiful and so vulnerable.

Poor Francis, he had probably been alone all evening while she was away philandering with a married man. She could not for the life of her imagine what he was doing with matches all over the place, but she thought that whatever he was doing he must be lonely, insecure and unhappy, and he did depend on her so.

'Oh Francis,' she said, 'I'm sorry I'm so late. Really sorry.' And she was.

'Well, I'm glad to see you now,' said Francis and got up from the table and came to kiss her.

'Phew,' he said. 'Where have you been? You smell of frying.'

'Oh dear,' said Claire, taking off her coat. 'It must be the family I've been visiting, they were frying fish fingers.'

Francis went back to the table and began to fiddle with glue and matches.

'Do you mind if I have a bath before we eat?' she asked. 'I'm exhausted and feel filthy.' She wasn't in the least bit hungry.

[157]

'That's fine by me,' said Francis, engrossed in fiddling with his matchsticks.

'So what have you been up to?' she asked as she went away to run a bath.

She thought he replied, 'Making a model of Buckingham Palace,' but she supposed she must have misheard . . .

CHAPTER XIV

In the days that followed, Claire grew more and more tense and, as a result, increasingly irritable with Francis. She couldn't stop thinking about Gary and yet she was deeply concerned about Francis.

Months of inactivity seemed to be taking their toll on him. He was becoming almost stupid. How could he possibly think, for instance, that he could make a model of Buckingham Palace out of matchsticks with only one small photograph of the front of the building for guidance? His hopelessness was becoming increasingly annoying. Why couldn't he go out and get a job – or at least try – any old job? After all Gary had been out of work for ages and he had far more to worry about than Francis, and yet he wasn't limp and hopeless. He had even found a job now. Besides no one would ever employ Francis if he didn't look a bit more positive – like Gary – and walk with a spring in his step – like Gary.

She shrugged her shoulders irritably as she thought of Francis's feet. They were the most annoying feet she had ever seen in her life. No wonder he couldn't walk with a spring in his step.

Poor Francis. It was hardly his fault that he had annoying feet. She began to feel guilty about her irrational behaviour which was probably hurting Francis anyway as he must sense that her feelings towards him were changing. But what on earth should she do? There was no doubt about it that after living with Francis for five years, she owed him all her loyalty and, in any case, he needed her. What on earth would he do without her? she wondered.

Then she thought of marriage again. She now knew that she could never marry Francis. The awareness of that knowledge had been growing in her over the past days, but she had no notion of how she could ever tell Francis who, at any rate, seemed to be in no hurry to marry but who, she supposed, presumed, as she had done up to now, that inevitably the two of them would eventually end up married. She just hoped that he wouldn't bring the subject up again yet, although Christmas was drawing nearer and when they came home from their holiday in Italy they had more or less decided to announce an engagement at Christmas.

Claire was sitting in the kitchen having a cup of tea before leaving for work. She had woken early and had not bothered to wake Francis. She needed to be alone to think. She looked at her watch and saw that she still had plenty of time. Perhaps she would take Francis a cup of tea, but she hesitated. She couldn't face another conversation about what he was going to do that day.

She was fiddling with a packet of Francis's cigarettes which he had left on the kitchen table. She really felt like having one. She took a cigarette from the packet and glanced around for some matches. She couldn't think what had come over her. It was quite unlike her to smoke in the morning and for that matter she didn't think that she had ever smoked on her own before. Never mind. She was so tense these days and the cigarette would help her to relax.

She was enjoying her cigarette when she suddenly remembered that she had picked up the post as she went out the morning before and the letters were still in her bag. She had better have a look at them and see if there was anything important.

[160]

She delved in her bag and brought out two brown envelopes – a gas bill and something from the DHSS for Francis – and a handwritten letter addressed to Francis.

Francis didn't get many letters, so she wondered who on earth it could be from. She peered at the smudged postmark which seemed to say 'Derby'. That was where Francis's father lived. She wondered what on earth he could be writing about. Perhaps she would wake Francis after all.

Francis was fast asleep and it took some time to wake him up. When he was finally roused he said,

'Is there a cup of tea for me?'

'There's a letter from your father,' said Claire, 'and if you can be bothered to come into the kitchen, I'll make you some tea.'

'What's the matter with you this morning?' said Francis.

'Come on then,' said Claire as she disappeared back to the kitchen.

It was probably about two years since Francis last saw his father and their relationship was limited to an exchange of Christmas cards and perhaps two telephone calls a year at most. As for Francis's Christmas card to his father, it was usually bought and stamped and posted by Claire although he just managed to write, 'To Dad' and to sign his name inside it. Claire had no idea who bought or posted the card that came back. Perhaps Francis's father did it himself.

Francis came into the kitchen with Claire's dressing gown stretched and awkwardly tied round his meagre body. He had bare feet.

'Why don't you put something on your feet? They must be freezing,' said Claire as she put a mug of tea on the table for him.

Francis sat down and said, 'Where's the letter then?'

Claire handed him the letter. He took it and then spent some time squinting at the address and the postmark before turning the envelope around several times in his hand and eventually tearing it open.

He read it slowly and carefully without saying anything and then handed it silently to Claire.

[161]

He sipped his tea as Claire glanced at the sheet of paper in her hand.

'Dear Francis,' it read, 'I am just penning this short note to inform you that I have made a momentous decision which I feel sure will make me very happy. I don't think you have met Linda, but she is a very lovely person and we are to be married next week. After the wedding we plan to take a short break in the Caribbean and when we get back we would be glad if you could see your way to paying us a visit for a few days so that you can get to know your new "Mum"!

All the best,

Dad.'

When Claire looked up from the letter, Francis was lighting a cigarette with a trembling hand. He looked very pale.

'Will you go?' she asked. 'I think you should.'

Francis was furious. He hadn't seen his father for two years. He didn't care a damn who his father married or didn't marry and he saw no reason why he should bother to displace himself to celebrate the occasion. What was in it for him? His father had never done anything for Francis, why should Francis bother about him? And what the hell did he mean by Francis's 'new Mum'? Francis had had one bad mother. He didn't need another. His father had run through a series of mistresses over the years and Francis wondered what was so special about this one that he was going to marry her. It probably wouldn't last anyway as nobody could put up with Francis's father for long.

Claire was thoughtful. It would probably be good for Francis to go away for a few days. It might jolt him out of himself and besides Claire herself could do with the breathing space.

'I'd go if I were you,' she said.

'I'm not going without you,' said Francis.

[162]

'But I'm not invited.'

'Of course you are,' said Francis. 'It's obvious. He'd never dare invite me without you. Anyway, he likes you.'

'I've only met him a couple of times and, if you remember, he blamed me for you not working at university, so I doubt very much that he likes me.'

'Of course he likes you,' said Francis emphatically.

'Well, let's think about it and discuss it this evening,' said Claire. 'I ought to be going to work now.'

'And I'm glad he can afford to take a break in the bloody Caribbean,' said Francis, suddenly growing angry again. 'How does he manage to be so fucking rich while the rest of us starve?'

'Perhaps he works for his living,' said Claire tartly, as she put her dirty breakfast things in the sink.

'It's hardly my fault if I'm unemployed,' said Francis, 'so there's no need to be nasty. And if I did work for my living and if I had enough money to go swanning around in the Caribbean and if I had a son who was on the dole, I would help him out and be a bit more generous and give him the odd hand out.'

'Look here,' said Claire, pulling on her coat, 'if you never speak or write to your father how can he have the faintest idea whether or not you're on the dole? But if he ever saw you, it might be different – he might take more of an interest in you. Anyway at least that letter was meant in a friendly way. Now, I really must be off. Think about it and we'll talk this evening.' She picked up her bag, kissed Francis quickly on the cheek and left the flat.

Francis did begin to think about it. There was something in what Claire said about him never seeing his father who had clearly reached a point in his life where he genuinely wanted to make friends with his son again, and the occasion of his marriage just made things easier – a sort of excuse for getting in touch with Francis again. For all Francis knew, his father would be delighted to help him once he knew how badly things were going. He certainly wouldn't think it right that the woman in a couple should be the principle breadwinner – or rather the one with the money as it were. No, perhaps he ought to go. Not just to try and get money out of his father or anything sordid like that. No of course not. It wouldn't even enter Francis's head to visit his father just for the sake of what he might get out of him.

Claire was right. The letter had been sent in a friendly way and there was no point whatsoever in being churlish about it. Being churlish wouldn't get anyone anywhere and besides it would be quite wrong to refuse the hand of friendship.

Francis thought that by the time Claire came back in the evening he would be able to persuade her to come to Derby with him as he was sure that the invitation must include them both.

He had forgotten for the moment quite how violently anti-Claire his father had been when he and she first moved in together. He had gone on and on about bloody philandering and about how damn silly it was to settle down so young. He had called Claire a harpie and blamed her for seducing Francis and taking the lad's mind off his work.

He, Francis's father, had come up from nothing – his father had been down the mines – he wouldn't have got where he was without hard work. Somehow it seemed that Francis wasn't preparing to step in his father's footsteps. Bloody effete private school he'd gone to. That was what had spoiled the boy for work. Francis's father regretted every penny he'd spent on educating his son. He'd wanted to do well by the lad, but he'd ruined him. He should have gone to a proper state school with ordinary kids, then he might have learned to get off his backside and put his mind to something useful.

What with his privileged education and then the harpie coming along to seduce him, it was no wonder that Francis sat back waiting for money to fall into his lap. Francis's father had his mind made up about one thing and that one thing was that he wouldn't give the boy another penny farthing, not even if he were starving in the gutter. It

[164]

wouldn't be kind; in fact it would only make him lazier than he was already.

An hour after Claire left Francis was still sitting at the kitchen table with a cold mug of tea in front of him, wondering how the visit to Derby would turn out. It might even be quite fun. Francis hadn't been home to the Midlands for years and his father had moved house since then. He wondered what sort of a house he lived in now. Pretty comfortable, he imagined, perhaps there was even a swimming pool. Not that anyone would be wanting to swim at that time of year.

Francis's father had his own company, making nuts and bolts and screws and parts for agricultural machinery. He had quite a lot of business contacts all over the country and it even occurred to Francis that he might be able to find his son a job in London or somewhere nearby. Suddenly Francis rather fancied himself as a businessman. He began to envisage flying first class around Europe with an expensive briefcase under his arm – he would probably have to go to Germany and Scandinavia. Certainly Scandinavia. His father was always popping off to Oslo for a few days, he had a lot of dealings in Norway. Really the sensible thing for Francis to do would be to learn Norwegian. He could get some tapes or a Teach Yourself book. He might do that this afternoon. That was the sort of initiative which would definitely please his father.

He had really only initially rejected the idea of going into business as a kind of reaction against his father. But of course he was older now and he could see that he was probably quite like his father in some ways, so he had more than likely, inherited his father's flair for business. On the whole things were suddenly beginning to look quite rosy. He didn't think he'd go back to bed this morning. He'd make an early start for a change. After all, when he was a businessman he would have to start work at a reasonable time. Be up and about.

Francis liked the idea of his new sensible future and he was sure that Claire would like it too. She had laughed at him when she found him trying to make models out of matchsticks which had annoyed him at the time although he had realised pretty soon that he had started on far too ambitious a project with Buckingham Palace. He'd thrown all the matches away in the end.

He was just wondering how to spend the day when the telephone rang.

He was surprised and annoyed to hear Danny's voice at the other end of the line.

She was still looking for Roddy. Had he turned up yet? She must know. There was trouble waiting for him when the swine did eventually show his face. Big trouble.

Francis said that neither he nor Claire had heard anything from Roddy lately.

'You get in touch as soon as he surfaces,' said Danny menacingly. 'He's taken my credit cards too,' and she hung up.

What the hell was the matter with Roddy? Francis wanted to know. Always after money. Well one thing was certain and that was that when he, Francis, had made his fortune in business, he wouldn't give so much as a fiver to Roddy. Roddy was the sort who just expected money to fall into his lap and if he was given it it would only encourage him to be lazier than he was already.

Claire drove to work by way of Thackeray Buildings which added five or ten minutes to her journey.

It was several days since she had had tea with Gary and she longed to see him again but knew that if she did she would be courting disaster. She half wanted to call on the Flacks, because she knew she should, to see if Alma and the children were back, but she sort of knew that they wouldn't be back and that she might find Gary there alone again.

Of course Gary had a job now and she could perfectly well call during the day when he was at work, but somehow she didn't choose to do that. She knew she was being silly driving a long way round just in the hopes of catching a glimpse of Gary crossing the road or something. She was behaving like a stupid teenager and she should be ashamed of herself. But at the same time she wasn't really doing any harm, just looking at the outside of Thackeray Buildings.

She reached her office a few minutes late to find Barry, her team leader, wanting a word with her.

Barry would like to know if anything was worrying Claire. She was one of the best members of his team, but lately she seemed to have been slipping up a bit – not getting things done, arriving late, forgetting things. All this was uncharacteristic and Barry wanted to get to the bottom of the trouble.

He looked so concerned.

Suddenly Claire burst into tears. Everything was getting on top of her. But it would all be all right – she would try to manage, she would get herself organised.

'I'm terribly, terribly sorry,' she sobbed, as she blew her nose into a crumpled Kleenex.

Barry had left his desk and was standing beside Claire with his arm around her shoulder.

Claire wished he would go back to his desk and sit down because it only made her cry more having him standing there so sympathetically with his arm round her.

'It's just that I have a few personal – family problems,' she snuffled. 'Nothing that I can really talk about. It'll sort itself out and I'll be all right.' Then she began to apologise again.

At last Barry went back to his desk and sat down.

Claire blew her nose again, straightened her shoulders and pulled herself more or less together. She felt awful. She had been letting Barry down.

Barry told her not to worry and wondered if she would like to take a few days off and have a little rest. He didn't want her cracking up. The whole team would be lost without her.

Claire was flattered by Barry's compliments and gratified by his offer of a few days' holiday, but she was so behind with her work that she felt that it would do her more good to catch up with that than to hang around at home doing nothing. She didn't add that the idea of spending several

[167]

days with Francis at the moment was not one which appealed to her. The weekends were bad enough, but usually at the weekends they saw her parents or friends which helped them to ignore the growing tension between them. If she took days off during the week, everyone else except Francis would be at work and she and he would be thrown together in a way which she could hardly face at the moment.

'We'll see how things go,' said Barry, 'and just remember that if ever you do need someone to talk to, I'm always here.'

Claire thanked him and got up to go, apologising yet again.

'And Claire,' Barry said, as she reached the door, 'if you do change your mind in a couple of weeks or so, and you feel like a break, just say so. We'll count it as sick leave.'

When Claire got back to her own desk, puffy-eyed and snuffling, she sat down and spent the next six or seven minutes just staring into space. All her papers seemed to be in such a muddle and she knew that before she did anything else she really must clear her desk. And in order to do that quickly and efficiently she must put everything else out of her mind, but these days, however hard she tried, she could not forget Francis or Gary – Gary or Francis for more than a few minutes at a time.

Gary she loved and longed for. Francis she pitied and was beginning almost to hate. No, surely she couldn't hate poor, beautiful Francis. That was too unkind. Besides if she hated Francis it was entirely her own fault because she had failed him. Failed to help him and give him the support which he needed. Failed to convince him that she believed in him. Poor, poor Francis.

During the course of the morning, despite her wandering thoughts, Claire did manage to get a certain amount of work done. She didn't think she had any urgent calls to make in the afternoon, so she decided to get on with her paperwork. She might just try calling on the Flacks again before she went home, but on the other hand she might just not.

[168]

Towards the end of the afternoon she made a few telephone calls and then, as it began to get dark, she looked at her watch. It was nearly four thirty. If she left now, she would get to Thackeray Buildings before Gary came home from work and she could make a perfectly innocent routine call to see if Alma was back yet. If she wasn't, Claire really would have to get in touch with the social worker who had tried visiting Alma's mother. She would have to try again. After all, the child Yolande must have missed quite a lot of school by now.

Yes, it would be quite wrong of Claire to put off the call any longer. She had no right to put her own private problems before her job.

She would just make a couple more telephone calls and then she would be away.

Just as she was putting her coat on, Barry came into the office.

'You off now, then?' he asked.

'I've got a visit to make before going home,' said Claire.

'Good girl,' said Barry. 'I was just coming to see how you'd been getting on today. Everything all right?'

Claire explained that she had managed to get quite a lot done. She thought she would soon be on top of things again.

Barry patted her on the shoulder, complained about the bitterly cold weather and told her to keep her chin up.

'Don't be got down,' he said as she disappeared through the door.

Barry was really kind. A great support.

By the time Claire reached Thackeray Buildings, it was quite dark and very nearly five o'clock. Well, she hadn't looked at her watch, but she thought it must be getting on that way.

She banged on the door several times quite loudly but there was no answer and not even a squeak from the nosey neighbour. It was with a certain amount of relief that she finally gave up and turned to go back down the stairs. Just as she reached the ground floor a shadowy figure in a donkey jacket loomed out of the dark and she heard Gary's voice say,

'Hello luv. You coming to tea with me?'

'Oh, er,' she said nervously, 'are you back from work already? It must be later than I thought. I was looking for Alma.'

'Were you?' There was a note of incredulity in Gary's voice as he caught hold of her arm and swung her round to walk back up the stairs. 'Well, I'm afraid she's not here so you'll have to make do with me. Come on in and have tea.'

As Claire allowed herself to walk back up to the flat with Gary her knees felt like water and her heart was pounding so fast that she thought he must be able to hear it.

When she left Thackeray Buildings again a couple of hours later she was in a complete dither. She had no idea what was going to happen next – she could, she supposed, just take a grip on herself and make sure that she never saw Gary again, but somehow she knew that that was impossible. She must see him again and as soon as she could. But where would it all end? She felt wonderfully happy and then instantly plunged into gloom as guilt about Francis swamped her.

She felt guilty about Francis and she felt guilty at having behaved so unprofessionally. She had let Barry down and to a certain extent she had let Alma Flack down. She had only seen Alma once and she remembered that she had felt genuinely sorry for her. Alma was the sort of woman whom Claire felt a real urge to help. Someone who had been completely overwhelmed by circumstances and who with some help might be able to cope more easily with her lot.

It was really in order to help women like Alma who had never had her advantages in life that Claire had originally become a social worker and she hoped and supposed that perhaps she had sometimes managed to make things a little easier for one or two of them. But even if Alma's marriage, which was based on a teenage mistake and Gary's affection for his children was in a bad way, there was no excuse for Claire to make it worse by having an affair with Gary.

She shook her head as though to clear her mind as she drove home through the evening traffic.

It was raining in fits and starts so that she had to keep turning the windscreen wipers on and off.

Oh God, what had she done? She had made things much worse than they were this morning and now she longed even more fervently for Gary but before she could see him again she had to face Francis and spend the evening and the night with him and with her guilt gnawing at her heart.

When she opened the door to the flat she heard Francis talking in the sitting room.

She stood on the landing holding the front door open and listening.

Who could he be talking to? She didn't really feel like seeing people this evening.

He was talking very quietly and in a silly voice. What on earth was he saying?

It sounded like, 'Hor manyay Nordmen bore in America,' and then 'Hor manyay Nordmen bore in England.'

She shut the front door behind her and went into the sitting room. Francis was quite alone, sitting on the sofa, staring at the wall in front of him with a book open on his knee.

He looked round suddenly.

'You came in very quietly,' he said, 'I didn't realise you were here.'

'What on earth are you doing now?' Claire asked. 'I thought you were talking to somebody.'

'I'm learning Norwegian,' said Francis. 'I went down to W H Smith's and got this book.' He waved the book at her. 'It's brilliant. It's just like English, I'll learn it in no time.'

Claire simply collapsed into an armchair, dropped her bag on the floor and stretched her legs out in front of her and sighed.

'Well good luck to you,' she said flatly.

'No, listen,' he said, 'When you came in, I was saying "*Hvor mange nordmenn bor i Amerika?*" which means, "How

[171]

many Norwegians live in America?" But I've learned millions of other words today.'

Then he started talking in a silly voice again and Claire felt like screaming or throwing something at him as he went on and on, reeling off his new found vocabulary.

'*Kake, undertøy, egg, lang, ung, tung, billig, lykkelig, flink . . .*'

CHAPTER XV

By the time Roddy was fifteen he had had more than enough of school and school had had more than enough of him. He would be able to leave immediately he had taken his 'O' levels but there was considerable doubt as to whether he would manage to pass many of them.

Nancy and George were in despair, trying to think what he should do next, – besides, the abortion incident had thoroughly thrown them both. Roddy was to a certain extent quite out of control. The school leaving age was due to be raised to sixteen over the next couple of years, but as Roddy and school were clearly incompatible, that wouldn't really have solved the problem.

In the event he spent two years after leaving school doing the odd job at local garages and newsagents, usually being sacked and generally getting into a number of scrapes.

George was irritated by his son's appearance – his long unkempt hair and bell-bottom trousers. He couldn't help thinking that Roddy's messy appearance was a reflection of his messy mind and that somehow, if only he could tidy himself up a bit, he might be able to organise his life better too.

But there was nothing the boy appeared to want to do. Whenever he was not working, he disappeared with groups of friends – to go heaven only knew where and do heaven only knew what – or he lay on his bed in his room listening to loud pop music.

Nancy thought that Roddy's hair and trousers were the least of his problems. All young people seemed to look like that in those days. She was much more concerned by the fact that she suspected him of dabbling in illegal substances. George agreed that this was probably the case, but neither he nor Nancy could either prove it or prevent it. They just had to wait patiently for the boy to grow up, come to his senses and find a purpose in life which they hoped would happen before any major catastrophe occurred.

Sometimes when she was alone, Nancy would let a silent tear fall. Where had she gone wrong? How had she failed Roddy? Was it really all her fault that he was such a hopeless person?

George had been a good father, perhaps a little strict at times, but otherwise kind and interested in his children's welfare. He couldn't be to blame. But had she loved Roddy too much? Spoiled him too much, or loved him too little and failed to understand the key to his character? Had those dreadful words spoken when he destroyed the tulips destroyed him? Had he discovered his mother's infidelity and had it marked him forever? She tortured herself endlessly, but could find no solution. Although she sometimes had difficulty in doing so, she still nurtured hope. Roddy was only young – youth was on his side.

At times Nancy longed for Roddy to be out of the house – away from the town where they lived. Even out of the country. Somewhere else, so that she didn't have to think about him and worry about him all the time. But she was appalled by such thoughts. How could she want to be rid of her own son whom she loved? She must be a very bad mother.

By the time Roddy was eighteen and had frittered away three years since leaving school, George decided that something must be done. The boy must be sent abroad. George had been patient but he could stand it no longer. He could see that Roddy was wearing his mother down, taking everything she gave as though it were his due and giving nothing in return. He was supercilious, selfish and lazy and he must be made to stand on his own two feet.

George bought a one-way ticket to Australia which he gave to Roddy with a cheque for £350 and told him to come home when he had seen something of the world.

Roddy was delighted. He couldn't believe his luck. He was thoroughly fed up with hanging around the same old dump all his life and quite surprised by his father's sudden generosity. Probably the old bugger just wanted to be shot of him, but it was pretty decent all the same. For once he thanked his father with something vaguely resembling genuine gratitude and left home without a care in the world.

He was away for over two years. God only knew what he got up to during that time. Nancy and George both felt in their hearts that the less they knew the better, but Nancy couldn't help but weep over the lack of communication. During the whole two years that Roddy was away his parents only ever received two postcards from him. One from Sydney and one – months later – from Changmai in Northern Thailand.

It was true, to a certain extent, that with Roddy away Nancy stopped worrying about him but there was always a weight in her heart and with his disappearance she became a quieter and sadder woman.

But she drew comfort from her daughter, Claire, who was, in contrast to her brother, a child of whom any parent could be proud. She did her work at school without too much fuss; she had nice friends and was helpful, friendly and generally good natured. And in addition to all this, she knew what she wanted to do, so she had a purpose in life.

During the years that followed, Nancy continued with her work for charity devoting more and more time to it; she kept house, concerning herself with the welfare of her family but sometimes, when she stopped to think, it occurred to her that life had passed her by.

[175]

She wasn't really sure what she meant by that since she realised that all over the world there were people – billions of them – whose lives were no more interesting than her own. Perhaps she was just growing old – and resenting it a little.

George, on the other hand, had moved uncomplainingly, even gladly, into middle age. He bought himself a dog to which he devoted a tremendous amount of attention and which he took for long walks, partly in order to exercise himself. If anything, he became more than ever settled in his opinions, more placid and contented than before. He didn't talk very much but spent hours, when not walking the dog, reading the papers, doing the *Times* crossword and snoozing to the dulcet – or, as Nancy thought, often jarring – notes of Radio 3.

Perhaps it was George's dullness or predictability which lay at the root of Nancy's idea that life had passed her by. There was no doubt about it that George was a good, hard-working, even-tempered man, but one who would never say or do anything to take anyone by surprise. He was set in his ways and had been since before Nancy even knew him. Sometimes she thought that what he really lacked was the faintest streak of fantasy.

It might have been this which led her to indulge her own fantasy so fully: George, of course, would be quite horrified were he to suppose that she mentally undressed the butcher, the baker and the greengrocer, that she dreamed of romantic encounters with Paul Newman, Michael Caine, the Shah of Iran and even Dr Kissinger – almost anyone who was in the news. But – she argued to herself – who was she harming? There had to be some spice to life.

When Claire, aged eighteen, brought home her first boyfriend, George was full of doubts, but Nancy was delighted. Claire had always been a studious and rather serious girl and her mother was glad to learn that she also had a social life. The boy was, Nancy agreed with George, a little on the wet side. But there was no harm in that, and he was, after all, her first serious boyfriend - so far as they knew.

Nancy watched them walking down the garden path hand in hand on a Saturday afternoon and felt a sense of relief and achievement. At least Claire was not beset by the guilt and doubt that had beset her in her youth. That at least was something to be glad about.

George was not so glad about that. He didn't know what the two of them got up to, neither did he care to dwell on it but just hoped that it wasn't much. He didn't approve of the permissive society. He had seen what permissiveness had done for Roddy and he didn't like it.

Nancy couldn't agree with him but she kept her opinions to herself, just hoping that no one would get too badly hurt.

In the event, it was the wet young man who was hurt when at the end of the year, Claire went away to university and quickly forgot about him.

One Monday morning soon after Claire had gone away, Nancy was tidying the sitting room. She picked up a Sunday newspaper which lay on the coffee table and was about to throw it away when she noticed a remarkably handsome photograph of Richard Burton.

Richard Burton was without doubt one of the world's most attractive men. His voice alone had the power to start Nancy daydreaming for hours. His pockmarked face and devil-may-care good looks were worlds away from George's neat, bespectacled, slightly wooden appearance. Nancy felt that she would happily put up with all the drunken tantrums and shouting just for one night in the great man's arms.

She stood in the middle of the sitting room with her duster under her arm reading yesterday's paper. Over the weekend Richard Burton had – in a mud hut in a Botswanan village – married Elizabeth Taylor for the second time. She had been wearing green whilst he was dressed in white trousers with a red shirt. Nancy tried to picture the occasion. Somehow Botswana didn't quite manage to capture her imagination and she didn't quite like the red shirt. Her affair with the wonderful, pock-marked actor would have to take place somewhere else – in the Ritz Hotel – no, she thought not, but perhaps in a windswept cottage on the Welsh coast . . .?

Suddenly the front door bell rang and Nancy jumped out of her skin as she always did when interrupted in her reverie.

Who, she wondered as she went to open the door, could it be at this hour? Richard Burton himself perhaps, already regretting his hasty remarriage and come to claim Nancy for his own. She smiled to herself as she turned the door handle.

'Good God, Roddy, is it really you?' She could hardly believe her eyes as she looked at her son standing there, brown and thin and older looking than when she had last seen him.

It was quite extraordinary to see Roddy suddenly walking through the door with a swagger as if he had never been away. Nancy was so overcome that she had to sit down.

Roddy had come straight from London Airport where he had landed a couple of hours before. The trouble was he might have to stick around for a while – until he got things sorted out. He was right out of cash, but he had several irons in the fire and would soon be in business again. But he had to wait for his partner to get back from the Far East.

Nancy wanted to know what sort of business. She wanted to know everything – where he had been – what he had been doing – how he had supported himself – was he well – he certainly looked well – happy – was he happy?

Oh, things had gone fine right from the very start. He'd met this guy in Sydney and they'd started up in business straight away.

But what sort of business, Nancy wanted to know.

Import, export – that sort of thing. To be perfectly frank, things had been getting a bit difficult Down Under lately so Roddy and his partner had decided to move their centre of operations. They were planning to make London their base from now on.

[178]

But what, Nancy wanted to know, were they importing and exporting?

This and that. Oriental trinkets, rugs, bracelets, anything really.

Nancy felt a thrill of deep pleasure, pride and relief at the thought that Roddy had at last found something to do and that he appeared to have confidence in his ability to do it. And he had apparently been supporting himself well enough for more than two years now. She only wished that he had written a bit more often. She had missed him dreadfully.

Roddy was amazed that Nancy hadn't ever got his letters. He'd sent letters from all over the world. They must have got lost in the post.

'Everything's upside down in some of those places,' he said by way of explanation. 'They've no idea about organisation. Probably never even empty the letter boxes from one year's end to the other.'

Nancy was quite satisfied by this but when she told George later he was more sceptical, although he didn't say much to Nancy for fear of upsetting her. He was also rather worried by what Roddy might be up to. He would like to know more about this so-called 'business'.

Roddy pointed out with a sneer that he didn't interfere with his father's work and he would therefore be grateful if George would refrain from interfering in his.

'If you are involved in anything illegal,' George said coldly, 'I would ask you to conduct your affairs elsewhere rather than in my house.'

Roddy gave one of his disarming smiles and chuckled.

'Come on, Dad,' he said, 'you know me better than that. Now would I be doing anything illegal?'

George hoped not.

Anyway Roddy wouldn't be hanging around for long. He'd be off to London as soon as Pat arrived. He hoped Pat wouldn't be delayed too long.

In fact Pat never turned up. There never seemed to be any very good explanation for his failure to materialise but

Roddy remained optimistic and before very long he was in touch with some contacts he had in London and had moved out of his parents' home to a flat in Tulse Hill. There he remained for some time, on the dole as far as his parents could make out, and then dabbling in second-hand cars. He came home infrequently, as often as not to try to borrow money from his father, and so life, for Nancy, became once again, very much what it had been before the magical moment of Roddy's return. Once again, there was a leaden weight in her heart, and when she did think of Roddy it was with a sense of her own failure.

Nancy tried not to think about Roddy too much, but to dwell instead on Claire's success and on her own easy relationship with her daughter which was a great comfort to her. Her relationship with her own mother who had died a few years ago now had been far from perfect – distant and in some ways almost non-existent, but she and Claire really did seem to get on well together.

Claire filled the house with her friends from university and was always cheerful and pleasant. During her last year she met a boy with whom she went out for nearly three years and whom Nancy was sure she would eventually marry. He was a nice boy, if a little ineffectual, but Nancy felt that he and Claire could be happy together and she had really grown quite fond of him by the time that Claire announced one weekend, with a long face, that she and the boy had 'finished'. She didn't wish to talk about it, but it was probably all for the best.

Nancy felt quite sad, and sorry for Claire who looked so down. Claire had been working now for nearly a year, and she had a nice little flat not far from where George and Nancy lived, but she was twenty-three, nearly twenty-four and Nancy felt that the time had come for her to settle down. Nancy would like to see her daughter married.

When Claire telephoned with a cheerful voice to say that she had met someone she wished to bring home and introduce to her parents, Nancy was thrilled. Perhaps this was it. The big thing. Mr Right. Claire had sounded so happy on the telephone.

Nancy busied herself all Saturday morning and most of the afternoon, preparing a delicious supper. She felt rather foolish, but she knew that she wanted to impress the young man, for Claire's sake – somehow she was sure that this was going to be 'Mr Right'.

She was glad for Claire that she had had some experience before settling down. Things were so much better these days – franker, more open, easier. Her daughter, she felt sure, had never suffered the traumas that she had experienced as a young woman and so would probably not find it necessary to go off in later life and be unfaithful as she, Nancy, had done.

George came into the kitchen with his dog padding faithfully behind him.

'What's all the fuss about?' he asked. 'Anyone would think Escoffier was coming to supper.'

'Who?' asked Nancy.

'Escoffier,' said George and suddenly began counting on his fingers. 'Of course it is,' he said, 'Oriental officers confused the cook, nine letters.' He turned to leave the kitchen again with the dog still padding behind him.

'I don't know what you're talking about,' said Nancy irritably to his retreating back.

'Eight down,' said George from the hall.

By the time everything was ready Nancy was in a ridiculous state of nerves.

'Have you got a bottle of wine, George?' she said. 'Open a bottle of wine.'

George thought that Nancy would embarrass the boy – frighten the poor fellow off if she went on making such a fuss. Nancy wasn't listening. She was wondering where on earth they would have the wedding reception. Their house wasn't nearly big enough. She supposed it would have to be in one of the local hotels. Claire would make a lovely bride.

'What's this boy called then?' George wanted to know.

[181]

'Francis,' said Nancy. 'Francis – but I can't remember what Claire said his surname was. It's a nice name, Francis – don't you think?'

'Boring,' said George mildly and returned to his newspaper.

'Oh, do open the wine,' said Nancy.

George good-humouredly put down his paper and heaved himself obediently out of his chair.

When Claire and Francis eventually arrived Nancy was quite amazed.

Francis was not at all what she had imagined. The funny thing was that Claire always seemed to pick what Nancy would have described as rather effeminate types.

Nancy hadn't really taken in what Claire had said on the telephone; she hadn't realised, for instance, that Francis was younger than Claire, still at university. She could no longer tell the age of young people but she would certainly not have put Francis at a day older than eighteen. He looked as if he hadn't begun to shave with his fresh young girl's complexion.

He was fair and thin with delicate features and a quiet apologetic voice – not that he spoke very much and when he did, he looked to Claire for approval. His movements were nervous and sudden and he chain-smoked, smoking even at table which Nancy regarded as bad-mannered.

Nancy was quite thrown out: this was not the son-in-law she had expected. But then who ever said that Francis and Claire were to marry? Of course she had been jumping the gun. How ridiculous of her. No, of course they were merely friends. Whatever made Nancy think that there was any more to it than just that?

Claire was her usual cheerful self. Gone were the gloomy looks and woeful sighs of recent weeks. Nancy was glad that she was happy and supposed that Francis was just a friend – companion – whatever – a sort of stopgap between boyfriends. Nancy sipped her wine and thought how wonderful it was to be young these days. How easy and pleasant people's lives seemed to be in comparison to before. They did what they liked without fear of judgment. But still, Francis didn't seem very attractive to Nancy.

So it turned out that Francis was still at university. In his last year, reading engineering.

George asked him what he wanted to do when he had finished his degree.

Francis lit a cigarette.

'I'm thinking,' he said with sudden emphasis, 'of taking up photography. My father's in business, but I can't say I like the life style. I would prefer to do something more creative.'

George was a little surprised.

'So you won't be using your engineering degree?'

No, Francis hoped to do quite well in his finals but quite honestly he had realised that engineering was not for him. Photography, he thought, was really much more his sort of thing.

'He's taken some wonderful photographs,' said Claire enthusiastically. 'You should see them – really brilliant still lifes in black and white.'

They took their coffee through into the sitting room and George was just giving a lump of sugar to the dog when Claire cleared her throat and said,

'Well, we think we ought to tell you both that we have taken a rather sudden decision . . .'

Nancy's blood ran cold. It wasn't possible . . .

'We've decided,' Claire went on, 'that we aren't going to get married . . .'

Nancy breathed again.

George raised his eyebrows and forgot to give the dog a second lump of sugar but held it still, just out of reach of the slavering animal.

'It's not exactly that we don't believe in marriage,' Claire said, 'but we feel that we're not ready for it.'

George couldn't believe his ears.

'But we are going to live together. In fact Francis has already moved his things into my flat.'

George lowered his eyes to the floor. He was embarrassed, but he would talk to Claire alone – later.

[183]

Nancy just said, 'Oh,' and then lamely, after a pause, 'I hope you will be very happy.' That sounded pretty silly and she couldn't think why she'd said it. Then she couldn't think of anything to add, for although she approved in theory of the modern way of life, she suddenly felt sad, let down, even bitterly disappointed. But she supposed she would just have to take this new development in her stride. On the whole Francis seemed a nice enough boy. Not ideal, but nice enough.

CHAPTER XVI

Claire was delighted when Francis told her that he had agreed to go and stay with his father, although she was not quite so convinced as he was by his future as a business-man. But somehow Francis's whole life plan – or lack of it – had ceased to engage her interest. She just wished he would shut up about it and she certainly wished that he would stop chanting ludicrous Norwegian words at all hours of the day and night.

Since deciding to visit his father Francis had taken to waking up earlier and in a brighter than usual frame of mind.

As Claire made the tea and toast in the morning he would bound into the kitchen on his long thin feet, saying:

'*Bok, hand, fot, vinter, sommer, finger, orkester,*' in what he thought was a perfect Riksmål accent.

He told Claire that two languages were spoken to this day in Norway. Landsmål and Riksmål. He was learning Riksmål, the most widely spoken language and the language of the capital.

Claire didn't frankly care which kind of *mål* he was speaking. One was probably just as idiotic as the other and it didn't seem to be a sign of great linguistic talent to be able to say 'finger' and 'instrument' in a sing-song voice.

Francis thought she was being unfair. She should be glad

that he had at last found something to do which interested him. But then Claire had changed lately. She was no longer her usual, sunny, loving self, and it was really because of this that he had finally agreed to go to see his father without her. Perhaps after a few days' separation they would be able to get on together better again. Besides he felt sure that when he came back with a job buttoned up, she would be thrilled and then she would realise that he hadn't been so silly after all when he started to learn Norwegian.

In fact he was learning it remarkably quickly which gave him a great sense of achievement and reminded him that, after all, he did have a brain in his head. He couldn't for the life of him think why he had ever toyed with the idea of making jewellery or building models with matchsticks. He was a thinking person – not a doing person. He even forgave the men in the Bricklayers Arms for laughing at him. They were quite right really. He wouldn't have got anywhere with that idea.

When he went to the Bricklayers Arms these days he greeted the regulars with a cheerful, sing-song,

'*God dag, god dag*,' and told them all about his plans and how his father was going to help set him up in business.

The men just raised their glasses, laughed and said, '*Skol.*'

Francis had never been so full of himself. Life really was about to take a turn for the better. He could even see that these last few years had possibly been a little difficult for Claire – not just for him. But once he had this job everything would change. He and Claire would probably even be getting married soon.

After a couple of pints Francis would leave the pub, waving a carefree hand and saying, '*Adjø, adjø; farvel, farvel.*' He had learned that greetings in Norway were thought to be more cordial if repeated twice.

Claire thought she must be going mad as the pressures on her became almost unbearable. Her guilt about Francis was bad enough in itself particularly as she now knew that they must part company, but to that was added her guilt about Mrs Flack – and her professional guilt.

[186]

Claire had reached the point where she knew that she could no longer bear living with Francis and she knew, too, that even if Gary were removed to a faraway land, she could never go back to having a proper relationship with him. She had lost her faith in Francis which seemed to her to be an almost worse crime than her sexual betrayal. How on earth would she ever be able to tell him that the end had come? Why on earth was he so stupid that he couldn't see it for himself?

Francis had had a cold for most of the autumn – there was nothing particularly new about that – but didn't he realise that a young man of his age ought to just stop having colds sometimes and find a little sexual energy? Claire supposed that she might be being unreasonable, but she didn't care, in her heart of hearts she knew she was right.

She wondered when Gary had last had a cold. He'd probably never had one in his life, or if he had, he probably didn't notice it.

Claire's work was suffering. She hadn't done anything about Alma Flack although she knew that the child, Yolande, had not yet returned to school. The schoolteacher had been on the telephone again, wondering if anything had been done to find the child.

Of course it didn't need the schoolteacher to tell Claire that Alma Flack and her children were still away as most evenings on her way back from work she had been calling on Gary in Thackeray Buildings.

Gary wanted to marry Claire which hardly made things easier particularly as he wasn't exactly free to make the suggestion.

Claire also wanted to marry Gary. And she wasn't really free either.

Claire knew that if Gary finally left his wife for her, the scandal would be overwhelming. She would probably have to give up her job and, when the truth was known, she might have difficulty in getting another one. She loved social work which had always given her life a sense of purpose and she had no idea what else she could do. She supposed she could always work in a shop.

Such was her passion for Gary that she believed she would be able to sacrifice her job and her conscience and suffer the humiliation of the scandal for his sake.

But what would the future hold? She tossed and turned at night beside the sleeping Francis, adding up the pros and the cons. The one and only pro, she knew, would be the freedom to love Gary openly – to live with him and to bear his children. On the other hand, she must face up to the fact that Gary came from an entirely different background, their friends were entirely different, they each had a different life style and even the expectations which they had of life were probably different.

Surely these things no longer mattered in the modern world. Class differences were outdated, Claire told herself. They could easily be overcome. Besides Gary was kind, intelligent, humorous, sensitive, caring – why, once they had survived the inital trauma of the scandal, should they not be happy together? Were their tastes really so very different? They both liked baked beans – and shared a consuming passion for one another.

But what when the passion died? Claire could not imagine it dying – and anyway, there would be kind, intelligent, humorous, sensitive, caring Gary.

In her heart of hearts Claire knew from experience that in matters of love people invariably did what they wanted to do in the end, regardless of any arguments designed to sway them towards the path of wisdom. So she knew that in the end she would have to tell Francis – Barry – her parents – the world.

But her thoughts returned persistently to the problem of how she could ever tell Francis. She would break his heart and shatter whatever remained of his self-respect.

When she thought of the path of wisdom it hardly seemed to indicate a lifetime with Francis. So she had, whatever happened, to leave Francis, but was she to deny herself Gary as well? If there were no Francis and no Gary –

[188]

what would become of her then? She could leave them both, hand the Flack case over to another social worker and wait – to meet someone else? But she would never meet anyone like Gary ever again.

And so she tossed and turned night after night, always putting off the moment of decision.

She would wait for Francis to go away to his father's and then she would have the freedom to think more calmly. She would reach her decision in his absence and decide then how best to break the news to Francis. She was at least relieved that he had so easily accepted to go away without her.

She became so tired and distraught that eventually she decided to take up Barry's offer of a few days off work. She would take them while Francis was away when she could be alone in the flat. Her work had been so disorganised lately that the office would probably be better off without her for a while.

On the evening before Francis was due to leave for Derby, Claire came home early. She was feeling really bad about Francis and had bought some steak for supper and a bottle of wine.

She came into the flat to find him sitting at the kitchen table with his Norwegian grammar book and an exercise book open in front of him.

He was saying out loud to himself as he wrote carefully in the exercise book,

'Seksti, sytti, 'åtti, 'nitti, hundre . . .'

He looked like a little boy and suddenly Claire forgot about his thin boney feet and was swamped with compassion as she gazed almost as though for the first time, at his delicate, sensitive profile and long, thick eyelashes.

She walked quietly up to him and tousled his hair.

'Dear Francis,' she said.

He turned and smiled a beaming happy smile, delighted to be back in favour again.

'Sexty, sitty, atty,' she said gaily. 'What a ridiculous language!'

[189]

She suddenly felt rather mean. Learning Norwegian was the first thing that had enthused Francis for a long time, and she of all people had longed for him to find something to interest him. Perhaps she was wrong and his father would find him a job. Perhaps he would learn the language properly and be sent to Oslo. She hoped so.

'How's it going?' she asked.

'Not so badly,' said Francis pushing aside his books and standing up. 'It's really quite fun you know.' Then he added, 'Hey, what's up? You're home early.' He looked at his watch, '*Hva er klokka?*'

'Oh Francis, please don't talk Norwegian to me.' A note of irritation had crept back into her voice.

'All right,' said Francis. 'No Norwegian tonight. I'll put the books away.' He had been so cheered by Claire's gentle manner when she came in that he felt he would do anything to keep her in that mood for the evening. After all he was going away in the morning. Only for a week but then they hadn't been separated for as long as that for years.

Claire was very quiet at supper. Sweet and gentle but quiet. She even looked rather sad.

She needed a rest, she said.

Francis talked about his hopes for the future. He couldn't see any reason why his father wouldn't help him. If he could get a proper job things would really change.

Claire said nothing but she remembered Francis's father, a greedy, hard, unforgiving man, and she thought no, after all, it's not very likely. She could almost hear him saying, 'Sorry, old boy, we don't carry dead wood.'

After supper they watched television, sitting side by side on the sofa. Claire wasn't concentrating – her mind was elsewhere. Later she couldn't even remember what programme they had been watching.

Francis held her hand. Afterwards, in bed, he made a move towards her.

'I'm sorry, Francis,' she said, 'it's just that I'm terribly tired.'

He leaned over her and kissed her goodnight.

'Never mind,' he said, 'I'll only be gone a week.'

He was soon asleep, but she barely slept at all that night.

In the morning her gentle mood had passed. She felt tense and wretched and irritable but decided that she must somehow control it at least until Francis had gone. She didn't have to go to work so she thought that when she had taken him to the station she would come back and go to bed. Perhaps she would be able to get some sleep.

Francis was in a complete panic. First of all he didn't know what to wear. He didn't want to make a bad impression on his father after so long, but if he dressed too smartly he would feel a fool. He was flinging socks and shoes and ties around the room, he couldn't find his toothbrush although he must have had it last night and where on earth had Claire put the razors he'd bought yesterday? He was sure he'd left them in the kitchen.

He went into the bathroom and clattered around in there for ages, packing his sponge bag. He mustn't forget his asthma pills – and it was always sensible to travel with aspirins – and some throat lozenges.

Anyone would have thought that he was going away for six months to the South American jungle – not to the Midlands for a week.

'When you're ready,' said Claire at last, 'we ought to go – or you'll miss the train.' She felt like death and her irritation was mounting.

'Come on,' she said, 'there's your Norwegian book on the table. Aren't you taking that?'

'Of course I am,' said Francis, snatching it up. He looked at it in his hand and said, '*bok, god bok*' before stuffing it into his case.

'Oh Francis, you're hopeless,' said Claire, 'you've left your wallet on the sofa, and there are a whole lot of socks on the floor. Do you want them?'

'No,' said Francis. 'I've got enough.' He put his wallet in his pocket and said, 'We must go.'

'Come on then,' said Claire. 'I bet you've left something else behind.'

[191]

'No, I've got everything now. Let's go.'

As Claire left the sitting room she caught sight of Francis's ventilator lying on top of the television.

She felt angry and tired and distraught and miserable.

For God's sake, she thought, can't he remember anything for himself? I'm not going to be here to look after him forever.

He'd got his pills, he could do without the ventilator. He probably wouldn't need it and, if he did, he'd just have to get another one.

She slammed the flat door shut behind them and they hurried down to the street and into the car.

Claire felt so tense that she nearly collided with a lorry as she moved out from the kerb. Then she crashed the lights and narrowly avoided knocking into a motorcyclist.

'Steady on Claire,' said Francis. 'What's the matter?'

'I don't want you to miss your bloody train,' she said between her teeth.

They just reached the station with only three minutes to spare. There was nowhere to park.

'I'll get out here,' said Francis, 'and thanks, I'm sorry I was in such a muddle.'

As he leaned over to kiss her good-bye he saw that she was crying.

He kissed her and squeezed her hand.

'Don't worry,' he said, 'I'll only be gone a week.'

'You must go,' she said, 'you'll miss the train,' and she squeezed his hand in return.

Francis got out to go, but came back for a moment, put his head through the car window and said,

'I love you. *Jeg elsker deg.* Let's get married when I come back.' Then he turned and ran for his train.

Hot tears rolled down Claire's cheeks as she watched the blurred, running figure of Francis disappear into the station. She supposed he hadn't forgotten his ticket which he'd bought the day before.

Then she remembered the ventilator.

Christ! What had she done?

She leapt out of the car and ran, stumbling and crying into the station, through the barrier, down the stairs, along the underpass and up the stairs to the platform on the other side.

'Francis,' she almost yelled as she reached the top of the steps, 'your ventilator!'

But he had gone and all she could see was the train gathering speed as it disappeared out of the station.

She turned and walked slowly back to her little green car which was standing in front of the station blocking the traffic, the engine turning, the driver's door wide open and with an angry traffic warden beside it.

When Claire finally reached home again there was Francis's ventilator still lying accusingly on top of the television. She wondered how soon he would realise that he had left it behind. Perhaps she should ring his father's house to warn him.

She dialled the number and waited for what seemed like an age and was about to ring off in despair when a woman with a foreign voice – perhaps Spanish – answered. Francis's father was out, this was the cleaning lady speaking, so Claire left a message with her, begging her to remember to pass it on, and then collapsed in exhaustion on her bed and fell into a deep sleep.

Claire slept on and off for most of the day and was woken in the middle of the afternoon by the telephone ringing.

It was Gary.

Alma and the children were back with Barry, the dog. Alma had told him to clear out. She didn't want to see him no more and she didn't want him coming round to upset the kids. As if he would ever harm them kids. He'd seen them and they looked all right to him. He thought Alma would send Yolande back to school now, but she had a wicked temper and Gary thought someone from the social services should go round and see her from time to time. He didn't want them kids coming to no harm.

Claire felt it was all too much although in a way she was half relieved. She told Gary to come round to her flat. He could stay there – Francis had gone away.

[193]

For the next twenty-four hours Claire and Gary existed in some kind of suspended state, oblivious to their worries and to the outside world. Bad weather had caused havoc in the building trade, so Gary had been laid off and was out of a job again.

They spent most of the time in bed, venturing out only to buy food and drink.

This blissful state of affairs lasted until nightfall when it was brutally interrupted by a telephone call. From the moment Claire answered it she knew that something terrible had happened.

It was Francis's father. He sounded as though he was crying. There had been an appalling catastrophe – a bit of an argument that morning about Francis's future – the boy had got rather worked up . . .

' . . .he was sort of gasping for air,' said Francis's father, ' . . .an asthma attack or something . . .' his voice broke, ' . . .we didn't know what to do. He didn't have his ventilator . . .hadn't had time to get another.' There was a long pause then a choking sound and Francis's father said, 'I'm afraid he was dead by the time the doctor arrived.'

'But what about the Spanish lady? I rang – didn't she tell you?' Claire asked futilely. There was nothing the Spanish lady could do now.

'Oh Maria – she only comes in once a week – never passes on messages.'

What were they doing talking like this about Maria when the world had come to an end?

When Claire had finished talking to Francis's father she turned and looked at Gary.

Would she ever be able to look at him again? No. While she had been 'honeymooning' with Gary in Francis's bed, Francis had died – killed by her – the perfect murder. But she knew as she stood there paralysed by the horror of the situation that she could never allow herself to benefit from the fruits of that murder. She was a murderess and she must bear that knowledge forever and take it eventually to her own grave.

[194]

'I must go to my parents' house,' she said dully.

Claire stayed with Nancy and George for some time. Nancy didn't know what to do with her – how to console her. She and George drove their daughter to Derby for the funeral and brought her home again, a broken contrite wreck. Nancy could not understand why Claire seemed to blame herself so for Francis's death. There was no reason for guilt. It had been a tragic accident and time would eventually heal the wound, leaving a scar – but the wound would heal.

But Claire's guilt was haunting. Nancy who had spent so much time dwelling on the subject of pointless guilt was quite appalled by the grip it held on her daughter. She had been so sure that she had made Claire into a balanced, happy person, equipped to deal with life's traumas without the added burden of the shame imposed so arbitrarily by society on its victims. But here was the living denial of all her hopes.

George was still talking about Original Sin. We are all born guilty he said. Neither principalities nor powers can change that. Some feel it more than others and those, he added in a sinister tone, that have no guilt at all are evil – born of the Devil.

'Tush,' said Nancy.

It was then they learned about Roddy. Nobody had heard from Roddy for weeks although they knew through Danny that he had been cashing her cheques all over London. He must, then, have gone abroad.

And indeed that was exactly where he had gone.

They arrested him at Kuala Lumpar airport with twenty grammes of heroin in his sponge bag. It would be a long, long time before he came home again.